EMERALD EYES

by

E. JAY HUTCHINSON

ISBN-13: 978-1530825356
ISBN-10: 1530825350

Published by

dizzy
emu
publishing

www.dizzyemupublishing.com

<u>EMERALD EYES</u>

EXT. BENSON, INDIANA - RURAL COUNTY FARM FIELDS - DAY

Crystal clear blue skies overlook acres and acres of plush
green fields, corn is knee high, gently sways in the breeze.

Swirl of dust trails behind faded red 1955 Ford Pick-up truck
traveling gravel country road. Truck slowly passes over small
quaint crescent-shaped concrete bridge.

Truck door painted in white letters 'Perkins Hardware' -
several fish swim upstream under bridge.

Truck creaks along approaches wooden Welcome sign.

'Benson, Indiana' - 'The Friendly city' it includes

'Home of the Bulldogs' - '1954 Baseball State Champs'

Bed of truck bounces as gravel road transitions to concrete
road leading to six local stores near the town square.

Tall silver metal flag pole in view, American Flag hangs
motionless, children's voices are heard.

INT. SCHOOL CLASSROOM - RIDGEVIEW SCHOOL - DAY

MRS. WEBSTER, 40, petite, pleasant looking, hair pinned up in
a bun sits at desk in front of 15 students.

                    MRS. WEBSTER
          Who knows who our first President
          of the United States was?

                    STUDENTS
          George Washington!

Most all of the children answer together but one boys voice
is heard the loudest.

                    MRS. WEBSTER
          Who knows the name of our second
          President?

TOMMY MARTIN, an excited blond haired 8 year old boy's face
oozes with confidence, eagerly waves his hand.

                    TOMMY MARTIN
          I know! I know!

Teacher's eyes scan the room, finds no one else. Kindly points pencil at Tommy, closest desk to hers.

> TOMMY MARTIN (CONT'D)
> John Adams!

> MRS. WEBSTER
> Very good, Tommy.

Laying pencil on book it slowly rolls off, over edge of desk. Tommy lunges, catches the pencil mid-air.

> MRS. WEBSTER (CONT'D)
> Nice catch Tommy.

> TOMMY MARTIN
> I play ball!

Proudly turning back he's mesmerized with LISA EVANS, an adorable auburn haired girl with pony tail at the next desk.

> TOMMY MARTIN (CONT'D)
> You got the sparkliest green eyes
> Lisa. Like emeralds.

Tommy's grin looks permanent staring into her green eyes.

> LISA EVANS
> Thanks Tommy...

> TOMMY MARTIN
> I hope we're in the same class next
> year too.

> LISA EVANS
> If we're lucky.

EXT. RIDGEVIEW SCHOOL - LATER

Children stream from school doors heading home, several walk toward school bus, circle Tommy.

> EDDIE
> Cubs are playing today.

> TOMMY
> Hope they win.

> TOMMY (CONT'D)
> Bye Bobby! See ya' Monday.

> BOBBY
> See ya' Tommy.

                         TOMMY
               Smell ya' later Ricky.

                         RICKY
               That's so funny I might laugh next
               week... if I remember.

INT. SCHOOL BUS - PARKED

Tommy cheerfully waves at BUS DRIVER, 50, bald, overweight,
cigar smoker as he races up the steps. Sits in the seat Lisa
saves for him.

                         TOMMY
               Thanks Lisa!

                         LISA
               What are you going to do this
               weekend, study?

                         TOMMY
               I gotta' practice. Schools easy,
               but baseball's tough.

                         LISA
               You're good at everything Tommy.

                         TOMMY
               I wanna' be a ball player someday.
               Maybe even play for the Cubs if I'm
               lucky.

                         LISA
               I'd go watch you play every day if
               you let me.

                         TOMMY
               I play for Perkins Hardware right
               now, we'll be playing at Hillman
               Park when summer league starts.

                         LISA
               By the Fire Department? I'll ask my
               mom if she can take me.

                         TOMMY
               I'll be with my dad, he's the
               coach. He can throw as hard as Ron
               Santo, my dad used to play third
               base too.

                         LISA
               Hope I can meet him.

Series of shots-

--Bus driver contentedly puffs on cigar traversing through
countryside dropping off random students.
--Tommy couldn't look happier sitting next to Lisa.
--Bus bounces over crescent shaped bridge seen earlier before
slowing, brakes squeal as bus stops at a cluster of homes.

INT. SCHOOL BUS - STOPPED

Emulating a traffic cop, hand help high, Tommy blocks off
aisle so Lisa can exit.

                    TOMMY
          Ladies first!

                    LISA
          Thanks Tommy.

                    TOMMY
          See ya' Monday Lisa.

                    LISA
          I hope so.

Bus continues to a dead end road surrounded by fields. Three
houses are visible, passing other two houses, bus stops at
the last house at the end of the road.

PEGGY MARTIN, 30, attractive woman long blond hair waits next
to hand crafted wooden mailbox, stained blue.

Bus door squeaks folding open.

                    BUS DRIVER
          Sure is a beautiful day.

                    PEGGY
          The flowers and yard could use a
          little rain but it...

                    TOMMY
          Look out below!

Tommy fearlessly leaps over four bus steps. Lands on loose
gravel, slides to a stop.

                    TOMMY (CONT'D)
          Safe!

Peggy's eyes widen clutching her apron.

                         PEGGY
            Oh Tommy Martin, please be careful!

Tommy dashes across the manicured lawn towards two story
house attractively painted robin's egg blue, dark gray trim.

Smaller color matching building stands alongside, both
decorated with beautiful flowers and trimmed bushes.

                         PEGGY (CONT'D)
            That boy is going to give me a
            heart attack.

He rushes up three concrete steps, front door slams as Tommy
disappears into the house.

                         BUS DRIVER
            Just a lot of energy but he's a
            real good kid on the bus.

                         PEGGY
            Thanks, we hope he's no trouble.

                         BUS DRIVER
            No trouble at all.

Driver puffs cigar, turns the wheel of the bus in the large
oval gravel area leaving a black cloud of diesel exhaust
fumes.

INT. LIVING ROOM - MARTIN HOUSE

Foil wrapped 'rabbit ear' antenna sit atop black and white TV
Tommy watches.

                         SPORTS ANNOUNCER
                    (on TV)
            Bottom of the fifth and the Cubs
            have a man on second. Here's the
            delivery...

INT. KITCHEN

Peggy holds bottle of coca-cola sitting down at sturdy well
used oak table, pulls lighter from apron, lights cigarette.

Timer sounds - "Ding"

She stands, removes pies from oven. Peggy tilts her head
toward living room.

                    PEGGY
          Oh, Tommy can't you go in your room
          and listen to that, you know how
          sensitive my ears are.

INT. LIVING ROOM

Tommy gladly leaps to his feet, turns off TV, dashes through
modestly decorated room.

                    TOMMY
          Okay Mom!

INT. BEDROOM - TOMMY'S

Lands on his bed, rolls over reaches for white transistor
radio, turns it on. Smiling, he listens intently.

                    SPORTS ANNOUNCER
               (on radio)
          The counts even at two and two with
          nobody out.

View rapidly passes over town several miles north to immense
body of water that has several industrial companies lining
the southern shore, including oil refineries and steel mills.

Miles up the shoreline to the west, the skyline of Chicago.

A "Crack" of a baseball bat is heard, a voice echoes -

                    SPORTS ANNOUNCER (O.S.) (CONT'D)
          Hard line drive - foul ball.
          Welcome again to the friendly
          confines of Wrigley Field for
          today's game with our beloved
          Chicago Cubs and the Pittsburg
          Pirates on this beautiful day the
          fourth of May nineteen sixty-five.

Standing out, a large steel mill with dark plumes of smoke
rising from smokestacks through-out the massive plant.

The Plant is loud the work hot, dirty and plenty dangerous
during the process. Multiple distribution lines of steel
rollers carry their product.

CARL MITCHELL, 30, chomps on wilted cigar, expertly operates
levers connected to control panel displaying a dozen green
lights.

INT. CONTROL ROOM - DAY

                    CARL MITCHELL
          This country is going to hell in a
          hand-basket. If I were in charge we
          wouldn't have to pay any taxes, I'd
          have a plan...

Behind Carl's back sits, LEE WARD, 30, horn rimmed glasses
rolls his eyes hearing this yarn numerous times before.

                    LEE WARD
          You know I'm voting for you Carl.
          Make me the Vice - President.

                    CARL MITCHELL
          Damn it I'm serious, just like this
          plant I'd have it running like a
          top and we'd all be making more
          money, if they just listened to me.

Lee lowers green hard hat over his eyes.

                    LEE
          I'm on your side Carl. I'm on...

A RED LIGHT unexpectedly appears on the control panel. Carl
looks to the wall clock layered with dust and grime. - 1:22

                    CARL
          Son of a bitch! Not today. I don't
          have time for this... Shit!

                    LEE
          Call the Millwright room.

Wall of the pulpit is covered with papers all shapes and
sizes, includes safety bulletins as well as department phone
numbers tacked up haphazardly.

                    CARL
          I'm calling the head honcho. I'm
          going to be so far up Highland's
          ass.

Carl's left finger stabs at the paper, lands on the listing
for Superintendents of Millwrights, his right finger
furiously dials the number.

                    LEE
          Be quicker to call direct.

Carl angrily snaps his head around.

                        CARL
            I'm in charge, we'll do it my way!

INT. MILLWRIGHT ROOM

Room's neat and spotless. Extra motors, gears and machine
parts extremely well organized on their shelves.

Alongside the door stands a 6' tall wooden cigar store style
Indian, a worker's tool belt hangs on it's shoulder.

Voice on Intercom - "Any body down there?"

JIM MARTIN, 30, confident looking man at the desk wears brown
hard hat uses curved metal tool, meticulously carves on a
block of wood resembling military tank.

                        JIM
            Hey Gene, so what do we owe this
            pleasure to?

                    GENE HIGHLAND
                (on intercom)
            Just got an ear-full, Carl's on the
            warpath, wants someone there asap.

Raising an eyebrow Jim turns toward the wooden Indian, slowly
turns to nearby table.

OTTO PARKS, 30s, large burly man fills out crossword puzzle.

                        OTTO
            Want me to take this one?

Teeth marks cover the faded yellow pencil Otto's sizeable
hand points toward the door.

                        JIM
            Not much room to work over there.
            I'll grab a white striper if
            there's any need.

                    GENE HIGHLAND
                (on intercom)
            Thanks, Jim. Out.

Jim removes the tool belt holding as assortment of wrenches,
screwdrivers and flashlight. THREE RED LOCKS hang from it.

Repeatedly rubs the top of the wooden Indian head.

                    JIM
               (toward wooden Indian)
          Look out for me Chief, don't let
          anything bad happen.

Pencil splinters in several pieces in Otto's hand.

                    OTTO
          Don't let Carl get to you, he can
          be a real pain in the keester.

INT. PULPIT

Door opens, Jim's head pokes in.

                    JIM
          Which line Carl?

                    CARL
          Over on two. Hey if you guys...

Door slams shut cutting Carl off, Jim walks around to the
rear of the pulpit.

INT. ELECTRICAL CONTROL PANEL

Jim pulls down handle marked #2, attaches red safety lock
through handle. He confirms, firmly pulls down on the lock.

INT. PLANT FLOOR - ROLLER LINE

Long greasy dirty line of steel rollers hold heavy iron
products at 10' intervals.

Line area remains extremely noisy from second line running
nearby, Jim inspects two damaged rollers.

Jim's eyes scan the plant floor, he sees two workers sweeping
floor wearing brown hard hats with a distinct white stripe
down center, he waves them over.

Approaching they look to be younger new workers with one
noticeably taller than the other, their clothes soiled with
dirt and grime.

                    JIM
          Okay, you're new so stay close and
          always focus on being safe. We need
          to go get two fresh rollers.

Passing pulpit Jim rocks backward, Carl unexpectedly opens
door.

                         CARL
              Now damn it Jim, I can't be late
              today. Helen works late shifts at
              the diner on Fridays and my boy has
              a dentist appointment at five.

Jim turns, spreads his arms wide.

                         JIM
              I've got a son too.

                         CARL
              Then quit wasting your time talking
              to me.

Pulpit door slams shut.

                         JIM
              Damn! That guy needs to slow down
              and smell the flowers. Gunna' get
              somebody hurt one of these days.

EXT. PLANT EMPLOYEE GATE - DAY

PLANT GUARD, 60s, thinning gray hair, sits on wooden stool
inside glass walled guard shack listening to radio.

                         SPORTS ANNOUNCER
                    (on radio)
              Ernie Banks got a hold of that one,
              it's in the right field bleachers
              and the Cubs now lead four to one.

Guard points to radio as dozen workers exit together at gate.

                         GUARD
              Go Cubs.

Walking alone Carl lights cigar. Remaining WORKERS surround
Jim.

                         WORKER # 1
              Have a great weekend Jim, got any
              plans?

                         JIM
              Got a few loose ends to tie up.

                         WORKER # 1
              A few more free repair jobs?

                  JIM
As long as Perkins donates the
materials the least I can do is
donate my time.

                  OTTO
Well damn it, give me a call. I
told you I'd give you a hand.

                  JIM
Perkins is the one who wanted to
start up a little program to help
out our community.

                  OTTO
What's on the list?

                  JIM
Well, two broken windows over on
Lake Street... a few shingles off
on Elm and some wooden steps for
the guy who had that shoe shop.

                  OTTO
Doesn't matter, at least give me a
chance to help.

Otto timidly grins pointing skyward.

                OTTO (CONT'D)
Maybe not the roof... don't think
it'll hold my big ass.

                  JIM
I'll see if I can come up with
something .

Carl attempts starting his rusty dented 1953 Studebaker
several times, engine finally starts in a cloud of smoky oil.

                  OTTO
Have a good weekend Jim.

                  JIM
Plan to Otto. You too.

Jim opens the door to his blue 1960 Ford pick-up truck.
Custom chrome exhaust pipes rise 5' skyward like a Semi-
trucks thru the bed of the truck, custom wheels and rims.

Grips the carved wooden baseball shaped shift knob, turns the
key. Engine roars to life on the first attempt.

"Vrooom - Vrooom"

EXT. BURR STREET - OUTSIDE PLANT

Studebaker smokes as Jim's truck easily passes it heading
home. Cigar as well as engine smoke fill the car, Carl scowls
as several more cars pass his car laboring to make the trip.

                    CARL
          Bastards, always in a hurry

INT. BEDROOM - TOMMY'S

'Tommy' unevenly written in ink across brand new Rawlings
baseball glove holding ball sits on dresser. Wall covered
with Cubs pennants and lots of baseball memorabilia.

Two shelves are loaded with over a dozen wooden carvings in
all shapes and sizes of animals to vehicles, includes five 6"
tall wooden letters. -T O M M Y-

                    SPORTS ANNOUNCER
               (on radio)
          Tie ballgame still in the top of
          the tenth inning, Cubs are letting
          this one get ...

                    PEGGY (O.S.)
          Gunna' be late.

He looks to clock - 4:47. Tommy leaps to his feet, turns to
door, takes 2 steps, turns back grabs glove and radio.

Races full speed through house.

                    PEGGY (O.S.) (CONT'D)
          So help me Tommy Martin, you slow
          down and be careful or I'll...

EXT. FRONT PORCH

Door slams behind Tommy preparing to sit on top step, his
eyes light up seeing Jim's truck pull in driveway. Sets radio
down, leaps off top step carrying glove.

EXT. DRIVEWAY

Jim's fingers mess Tommy's hair accepting his son's warm
embrace. Tommy takes several quick steps backward.

                    TOMMY
          Catch Dad!

Jim catch's ball barehanded, throws ball back while walking
backwards himself, toward smaller building.

                    JIM
          You're getting an arm on ya'.

After each catch Jim gets closer to building, stops at door.

                    JIM (CONT'D)
          Come on inside, I been looking
          forward to this, been a long hard
          week at the plant.

Door creaks open, exposes a meticulously organized wood
working shop with table saw, jig saw and drill press, various
woodworking tools.

INT. WORKSHOP

Jim walks past peg board wall to his right neatly covered in
dozens of hand tools, all tools outlined with black marker.

At back of room, 'Schlitz' - 'Pabst Blue Ribbon' signs adorn
the wall around refrigerator in corner, Jim opens fridge.

Tommy stops, admires the baseball trophy inscribed '1954
State Champs'. Displayed on the wall, black and white team
photos of Jim wearing his Bulldog uniform.

                    TOMMY
          I'm going to get one of these Dad.

Jim opens a cold beer, rubs the bottle across his forehead,
hands a bottle of coca-cola to Tommy.

                    JIM
          We were lucky, it takes a good team
          and lots of practice.

Tommy rubs the bottle on his forehead.

                    TOMMY
          I practice every day Dad.

                    JIM
          Always practice, lots of practice
          but it took a TEAM and a lot of
          luck to win that.

                    TOMMY
          I'm lucky Dad.

                    PEGGY (O.S.)
             Supper's ready!

Both their eyes open wide.

                    Jim
             Bet it's something good.

                    TOMMY
             I know it is, it was smellin' good
             before you got here.

INT. KITCHEN

Table's covered with fine country dishes, meat, corn,
cucumbers, salads and biscuits. Two pies are on the counter.

                    PEGGY
             How was your day Jim?

                    JIM
             You know stuff breaks all day and I
             have to fix it, never changes.

                    PEGGY
             That place is so dangerous I wish
             you'd go back to being a carpenter.

                    JIM
             You remember, it was feast or
             famine back then. The plant is
             steady and the benefits are the
             best.

                    PEGGY
             I sit here worrying about you all
             day long. I just wonder if it's
             worth it.

                    JIM
             It will be when I'm ready to retire
             and head out west to northern
              California. Just think what I can
             do if I get my hands on one of
             those big old redwoods or sequoias.

Attentively listening, Tommy inhales deeply distracted by
aroma of pies.

                         PEGGY
          Speaking of retired, Mr. Perkins
          called about material being ready
          for the Stenslav's. I wish you
          would charge for your time.

                         JIM
          That's why I help out, old man
          Stenslav had that shoe shop here
          for years, since I was a kid. Those
          are the kind of people that helped
          build this town.

                         PEGGY
          You're right, we do pretty good but
          you just seem so busy all the time
          and if some how you got paid for
          all your extra efforts.

                         JIM
          With the money we'll save by then
          and my pension when I retire from
          the plant. We'll do just fine out
          there. Warm, no more freezing
          winters.

Peggy's affection is undeniable gently kissing Jim's cheek.

                         PEGGY
          We are pretty lucky to have such a
          good life. When are you going to
          Stenslav's?

                         JIM
          Sometime tomorrow.

Tommy's concentration on pies is broken.

                         TOMMY
          What about fishin' Dad?

                         JIM
          Relax, we'll be there early, before
          they wake up and know what hit'em.

                         TOMMY
          We goin' to the big Lake or down by
          the river?

                         JIM
          I got other stuff to do later so
          we'll stay close by.

                         PEGGY
               Got room for one more?

The two look shocked at each other, Peggy smirks.

                         PEGGY (CONT'D)
               Just foolin', I know it's you're
               special place just be careful.
               Promise you'll be...

                         JIM
               Oh, he'll be fine Peggy, I won't
               let him out of my sight.

                         PEGGY
               I'm sorry, you know how I worry.

                         TOMMY
               Geez mom, I'm not a little kid
               anymore.

Peggy leans over kisses Tommy on his cheek.

                         PEGGY
               You'll always be MY little Tommy.

INT. KITCHEN - LATER

Peggy clears the table.

                         PEGGY
               Who wants pie? There's Dutch...

                         TOMMY
               Apple, with cinnamon!

                         PEGGY
               ... And peach cobbler.

                         JIM
               Can't ever beat your cobbler, a big
               slice for me.

Eating dessert together the family couldn't look happier.

EXT. MARTIN HOUSE - DAY

Gorgeous sunrise, birds chirp, two pheasant streak across the
sky behind workshop.

INT. BEDROOM - TOMMY'S

Tommy soundly sleeps, Jim pokes his head in room.

>   JIM
>   Gonna' be late sleepyhead.

Tommy springs out of bed, dresses in seconds, runs full speed
through living room almost beats Jim to the kitchen.

INT. KITCHEN

Peggy hands each a big fluffy biscuit with sausage patty,
slides several more into a paper bag, adds two red apples.

>   PEGGY
>   Now be careful Tommy, that water is
>   deeper than you think.

>   TOMMY
>   Aww, Mom.

>   JIM
>   It'll be fine Peggy, I won't let
>   those fish...
>   (chuckles)
>   Have Tommy for breakfast.

>   TOMMY
>   Sure Dad, you're so funny. Those
>   fish are scared of me, they try
>   jumpin' out of the water when they
>   see me coming.

Tommy stands taller, confidently looks at Peggy.

>   TOMMY (CONT'D)
>   It's for guys only Mom.

>   PEGGY
>   Don't other people fish there too?

Their pride's unquestionable looking at each other walking
out of the back door.

>   JIM
>   We kinda' marked our territory.

>   PEGGY
>   Well, you two have a good time.

>   TOMMY (O.S.)
>   See ya' later alligator.

INT. WORKSHOP

Black line is left showing the shape of the two fishing poles
Tommy removes from the pegboard.

Jim lifts old worn tackle box from under jig saw table.

EXT. DRIVEWAY

Focused on their mission they walk past truck, then mailbox
turn right.

                    TOMMY
          We going to have time to practice
          later? Little league starts in a
          couple weeks. Right?

                    JIM
          Sure does. We'll have all day
          tomorrow. Your first scheduled game
          won't be far behind that.

They follow uneven dirt path glistening with overnight
moisture.

                    TOMMY
          Dad... Dad. Remember you promised
          to take me to a Cubs game this
          year. You said when I got a little
          older.

                    JIM
          I believe you're right, you are
          older.

                    TOMMY
          I'm not no little kid anymore Dad.

                    JIM
          A promise is... a promise.

                    TOMMY
          Dad?

Jim's grins looking over his shoulder as he continues.

                    JIM
          Yeah...

                    TOMMY
          Dad!

Jim stops, sets down tackle box as he bends down on his knee.

                    JIM
          Just might already have a couple of
          tickets for the first week of June.
          Might be against the Cardinals if I
          remember correctly.

                    TOMMY
          You're the best dad... Dad.

Jim playfully messes Tommy's hair with his fingers.

EXT. RIVER BY CRESCENT BRIDGE

The two stand on a slight rise in the field, their house far
back in the distance several hundred yards. Together they
look down at the crescent shaped concrete bridge.

Two tree stumps sit side by side on the rivers edge, seats
and chair backs carved into them.

'Jim' neatly chiseled into one wood back, 'Tommy' is unevenly
scratched into the second.

                    TOMMY
          I like going to the lake but down
          by the river's my favorite.

Tommy casts his line as he jumps onto his stump.

Jim rolls over a large chunk of wood he previously fabricated
a table out of.

As Jim's sets lunch bag on table, Tommy's fishing line
tightens, he pulls back hard.

                    TOMMY (CONT'D)
          Got one Dad! Got the first one.

                    JIM
              (nods)
          Always do. I'll string him.

Jim struggles with wriggling fish.

As Jim slides the stringer into the water, Tommy gleefully
reels in fish number two.

                    TOMMY
          Better hurry Dad 'fore I get'em
          all.

EXT. RIVER BY CRESCENT BRIDGE - LATER

Suns bright rays on Tommy's face amplify the serenity he
quietly enjoys bonding with his dad.

Tommy suddenly flinches, a shadow momentarily covers his face
followed by another, several more shadows.

Startled, Tommy looks skyward. A dozen Canadian geese flying
low overhead.

Only their wings make any sound... "Flap, Flap, Flap".

                    TOMMY
          Holy cow those are big! Where you
          think they're going?

                    JIM
          They been south all winter, goin'
          back north somewhere's I imagine.

                    TOMMY
          To California?

                    JIM
          No, up north to Canada.
          California's out west. Where your
          mom and I plan to retire.

                    TOMMY
          I'm going too!

                    JIM
          We'll see, you might have plans of
          your own by...

                    TOMMY
          Where's Canada?

Jim casually points toward geese.

                    JIM
          Another country 'bout as big as the
          United States. Just follow them
          across the border and you'll hit
          Ontario.

                    TOMMY
          What's a border?

                    JIM
            Well, it's kind of an
             imaginary line that...

Tommy jumps to his feet on the stump, waves frantically at a woman and two young girls walking on the road over the crescent shaped bridge.

> TOMMY
> Hey Lisa!

> LISA
> Hi. Tommy!

> TOMMY
> I'm fishin' with my dad!

> LISA
> This is my mom and my cousin Cindy.

> TOMMY
> Hi Mom!... Hi Cindy!

Pointing to Jim, Tommy looses his balance.

> TOMMY (CONT'D)
> I better get back fishin' before my
> dad catches up, see ya' at school!

> LISA
> Okay. See ya' later!

He sits back down gushing.

> TOMMY
> She likes me Dad.

> JIM
> I figured as much.

> TOMMY
> I like her too.

Jim kneels down, water drips raising the stringer holding six brightly colored rainbow trout.

> JIM
> I'm bet you do, you're a good boy.
> Let's head back, got some chores.

> TOMMY
> Yeah, better leave some fish for
> next time.

> JIM
> Good idea.

INT. KITCHEN - AFTERNOON

Peggy removes a long polished serrated knife from drawer, raises an eyebrow. Jim lays the stringer of fish in sink.

> PEGGY
> Good thing you caught these because
> I didn't have anything thawed.
> Guess we would have starved.

> JIM
> It was mostly Tommy. I'm heading
> over to Stenslav's.

> TOMMY
> Can I go help Dad?

> PEGGY
> No! You stay here, it's too
> dangerous.

> JIM
> He'll be fine. I'm not on the roof
> or anything today, just some steps.

> PEGGY
> (to Tommy)
> Promise me you'll be careful.

> TOMMY
> Okay, Mom. I'm not a little kid
> ya' know.

INT. PERKINS HARDWARE STORE

MR. PERKINS, 50, distinguished looking gray haired man, neatly waxed mustache holds out glass container.

Tommy enthusiastically pulls out two sticks of red licorice as Jim picks up the materials for the steps.

> MR. PERKINS
> Really appreciate your help Jim,
> you too Tommy.

> JIM
> I decided on a name for our little
> project, Re-Build Benson.

> MR. PERKINS
> Sounds good, I'll order some shirts
> with your name sewn on the front.

Jim shrewdly looks at Mr. Perkins.

>   JIM
>   ... And YOUR store's name on the
>   back of those shirts?

>   MR. PERKINS
>   Little advertising never hurt.

Tommy smiles broadly chewing on a licorice stick.

>   TOMMY
>   My dad says at the end of a hard
>   days work, if you don't hurt a
>   little then you didn't try hard
>   enough.

>   JIM
>   That's a different kind of hurt
>   Tommy but it shows me you've been
>   paying attention.

>   MR. PERKINS
>   That's what I want to hear. You
>   keep paying attention Tommy. It's
>   going to be hard to find another
>   one like your dad. Maybe you'd want
>   to give it a try when you're older.

>   JIM
>   No offense Mr. Perkins but I'm
>   hoping for something a little
>   better for my son.

>   TOMMY
>   I'm gunna' play for the Cubs one of
>   these days.

Jim walks alongside Tommy towards the door.

>   JIM
>   That's sounds like a real good plan
>   Tommy. A real good one, I like your
>   thinkin'.

Mr. Perkins smiles watching Jim's hand reach toward Tommy's
hair.

>   TOMMY
>   Maybe you can be my coach there
>   too.

Jim's hand extends to Tommy's shoulder instead, pulls him
close as Tommy leans over.

EXT. FRONT PORCH - STENSLAV'S YARD - DAY

A small meager home, faded white paint with well worn porch
swing. Homemade rusty wind chimes hang from oak tree in front
yard, several homemade bird feeders as well in yard.

MRS. STENSLAV, 70, weathered face, wears long faded print
dress, black scarf over her hair. She never speaks a word,
hands glass of lemonade to each.

                    JIM
          Thank you very much.

                    JIM (CONT'D)
               (looks down at Tommy)
          Tommy?

Tommy hesitates sipping the room temperature lemonade.

                    TOMMY
          Thanks...

Standing noticeably hunch backed, MR. STENSLAV, 70, wears
dark slacks and well worn brown jacket with scattered holes
in it, shakes Jim and Tommy's hand.

                    MR. STENSLAV
          Tank you. Tank you for you help.

                    JIM
          Pretty sure I've got all the tools
          I should need. This shouldn't take
          too long.

Series of shots-

--Tommy closely watches Jim remove two rotting wooden steps.
--Watch's Jim sand and stain wood with perfection.
--Mrs. Stenslav expertly peeling potatoes on porch swing.
--Jim re-assemble steps.

EXT. STENSLAV'S YARD - LATER

Jim gathers tools, Mr. Stenslav stands next to Tommy.

                    Mr. STENSLAV
          You goot man Yim, you goot too
          Tommy. I gib you mooney.

Mr. Stenslav tentatively pulls out his wallet hoping Jim
refuses, Jim vigorously shakes his head.

                    JIM
          Don't even think about it. Our
          program helps out the people who
          helped this town out already. We're
          trying to pay you back.

Relieved, he slides his wallet back into pocket. Mrs.
Stenslav silently, not making eye contact holds out a plate
of oatmeal raisin cookies.

                    TOMMY
          Thanks!

Tommy eagerly takes two, cautiously takes two more.

                    TOMMY (CONT'D)
          I'll hold onto yours Dad.

Montage:

---Tommy in school happy and content always eager to
participate.
--Jim rubbing wooden Indian's head before leaving Millwright
room repairing various equipment around plant.
--Tommy waiting on the porch with ball and glove before
practicing catch with Jim in the yard after work.
--Peggy sitting at table drinking coca-cola's smoking
cigarettes waiting for pies in oven.
--Jim helping various town people in need in his spare
time... always with Tommy intently watching close by.

INT. PULPIT -

Red light begins flashing as Carl operates levers, he glances
at wall clock. - 2:24

Irritated, he grabs for phone, misses, tries again.

                    CARL
          Damn it! It those millwrights did
          their job like I told them to. I
          outlined a maintenance program for
          them to follow.

                    LEE
          Be faster if you called ...

Carl holds phone, looks directly at list of numbers on wall
dials Millwright room direct.

                    CARL
          Just gotta' be a smart-ass.

INT. MILLWRIGHT ROOM

Jim hangs up phone, looks over to Otto, walks toward tool-
belt hanging on wooden Indian, THREE RED LOCKS visible.

                    JIM
          Mr. Emergency. Got a roller down on
          one. Guess who?

                    OTTO
          Your favorite, the man that knows
          everything. Need help?

Jim attaches tool-belt, Otto never attempts to move.

                    OTTO (CONT'D)
          Just say the word.

                    JIM
          You take the next call, there's
          barely room for me under there.

Voice on Intercom - "Anybody down there?"

                    OTTO
          No friggin'... Jim's on his way
          already. Let me at that little
          pecker-wood.

Jim waves off Otto pushes door open with his shoulder.

                    JIM
          Be right there Gene...

In a hurry, Jim forgets to rub wooden Indian's head.

Stoic look on wooden Indian's face standing next to door.

INT. PLANT - ROLLER LINE

Arriving at line #1 with white stripers pushing cart carrying
three new rollers Jim removes tool belt to better fit in the
tight work area under the roller line.

Jim sweats heavily completing repairs, checks all surrounding
rollers. One additional roller in a precariously tight area
near end of line wobbles loosely in Jim's hand.

                    JIM
          Damn, this one won't last the
          shift.

Jim strains to crawl from under rollers, forms a plan looking
each worker up and down, points to taller employee.

                    JIM (CONT'D)
               (to white striper #1)
          You, go ahead to the wash house.
               (to white striper #2)
          ... and you, you follow me.

Taller employee walks away, Jim redirects shorter employee.

                    JIM (CONT'D)
          Got one spare roller over on line
          two. I'll get this one off while
          you're gone... save a little time.

INT. PULPIT

All panel lights are off, Carl impatiently presses start
button on control panel. No power.

                    CARL
          What the hell takes so long?

                    LEE
          Give him a chance Carl.

                    CARL
          I got deadlines to meet, those
          Millwrights could give a rats ass.

Carl notices white striper #1 walking past door.

                    CARL (CONT'D)
          Hey! Where you going, you finished?

                    WHITE STRIPER #1
          He said I'm done for the day, I'm
          heading for the lockers.

                    CARL
          ...'Bout damn time.

                    LEE
          Well hell, you don't need me then.
          I'm heading to the wash house too.

                    CARL
          Might as well, you only get in my
          way anyhow.

INT. ELECTRICAL CONTROL PANEL

Carl rushes past the employees, arrives at electrical panel only to see red lock, pulls down hard on it several times.

> CARL
> Bastard forget to take off his damn
> lock. I don't have time for...

Carl spins around gritting his teeth.

> CARL (CONT'D)
> More than one way to skin a cat.

INT. PULPIT

Carl jerks opens desk drawer, removes key chain holding dozens of random keys, hurries back toward electrical panel.

INT. PLANT - ROLLER LINE

Jim sweats heavily watching white striper return with new steel roller. Jim strains shoving existing damaged roller across floor. -   "Clang"

> JIM
> Be faster if you slide under here
> and hold it in place while I
> tighten it.

> WHITE STRIPER #2
> Sure, which way does it go?

> JIM
> I'll line it up you just keep it
> steady. Just be careful.

White striper struggles to get in confined area. Looks uncomfortable straining from weight of roller on his chest.

INT. ELECTRICAL CONTROL PANEL

Trying several different keys, Carl's eyes light up hearing distinct, "Click".

Sliding red lock into his back pocket Carl hustles back toward pulpit.

INT. PULPIT

Gratified look transforms Carl's face, he restarts line.

>   CARL
> Want something done, you gotta' do
> it yourself.

INT. PLANT - ROLLER LINE

Jim ears perk hearing the power being restored, understands dire situation. Shoves worker aside with all his strength.

New roller along with heavy metal products fall on Jim.

White Striper #2 frantically screams running up the line.

WORKERS hear screams, press safety stop switch located through-out the roller line.

"Alarm sounds" - Line lurches to a stop.

It's too late, Jim's crushed to death.

INT. PULPIT

Lighting fresh cigar Carl's face distorts. All red lights glow on panel.

>   CARL
> Damn it! Now what.

Carl leaves pulpit, charges down the line. He slowly eases up as he sees crowd gathered.

INT. PLANT - ROLLER LINE

>   CARL
> What's all this?

>   OTTO
> It's Jim, it's horrible. It's too
> late... he's gone.

>   GENE HIGHLAND
> Why in the world. Why wasn't this
> line locked out?

Gene desperately pulls on white striper's shirt collar.

                         GENE
          Did you see Jim lock it out? Didn't
          he lock out this line?

                         WHITE STRIPER #1
          I never saw him lock anything...
          Out.

                         CARL
          He musta' forgot, you know there's
          no way I could of ran the line if
          he did. Tragic, just... tragic.

Pale, sweating profusely Carl turns, walks away.

                         OTTO
          Bullshit! Jim was Mr. Safety he
          would never forget to do that.

INT. PLANT - ROLLER LINE- LATER

Plant floor is silent, Paramedics wheel Jim's blanket covered
body away. Several workers remove hard hats.

Otto slowly shakes his head, looks down at Jim's tool belt
laying along side the roller line.

                         OTTO
          You see what I see, Gene?

                         GENE HIGHLAND
          Jim's tool belt?

                         OTTO
          There's only two safety locks, just
          doesn't add up he always has three.

                         GENE
          Maybe... Hell, I don't know. This
          should have never happened.
               (angry)
          This never should have happened!
          Not on my...

Otto takes off his hard hat slams it against the roller line.

"Slam! Slam! Slam!"

                         OTTO
          Oh, Christ. Who's gunna' break it
          to Peggy? Oh, Christ!

EXT. FRONT PORCH - MARTIN HOUSE

Tommy sits on porch with ball and glove listens to transistor
radio. POLICE CAR stops in driveway.

POLICE OFFICER in uniform walks up looking uncomfortable.

>   POLICE OFFICER
>   What's your name son?

>   TOMMY
>   Tommy Martin.

Officer gently touches Tommy's hair.

>   POLICE OFFICER
>   Can you do me a really big favor
>   and stay right here so I can go
>   talk to your mom?

>   TOMMY
>   Sure!

Moments after the Officer enters the house a glass bottle is
heard breaking, Peggy's voice screams out in pain, cries out
uncontrollably.

>   PEGGY (O.S.)
>   Why? Why? I told Jim that place was
>   too dangerous. What about Tommy,
>   what's he going to do without a
>   father?

Tommy turns, his face saddens beginning to understand.

Turning back around Tommy's arm bumps the radio, it tumbles
down the steps, breaks into several pieces, radio's silent.

EXT. EVERGREEN CEMETERY - DAY

Looks as if the entire town has gathered. UNCLE BOB, 40,
tall, thin, professional looking man wears gray hat and
overcoat comforts Peggy. She wears black dress, hat, and
gloves.

>   PEGGY
>   Thanks for traveling from Michigan
>   Bob, we both appreciate it.

Peggy firmly holds Tommy against her.

>   UNCLE BOB
>   Sorry, Sis. Jim was such a good man

In the vast crowd are friends as well as numerous people Jim
helped out over the years, including Mr. Perkins.

> MR. PERKINS
> Jim was a great man doing so much
> for this town. Peggy, we will all
> be here for you and Tommy.

> PEGGY
> Tommy will need the most help, he
> was so close to his father, I just
> don't know what I'll do.

> MR. PERKINS
> Anything you need Peggy, anything
> at all... anything Tommy needs.

Walking away from the grave site Tommy sees people gathered
telling their own personal stories of how Jim helped them
out.

Tommy eyes turn toward ground with conflicting emotions.

INT. KITCHEN - MARTIN HOUSE

Peggy's eyes are bloodshot, her hand shakes smoking
cigarette, coca-cola bottle on table. Tommy leans against
doorway, stares down at floor.

> UNCLE BOB
> He should be here any minute, they
> better do right by you and Tommy.

> PEGGY
> I'm sure they will, it's a big
> company. Jim really enjoyed working
> there.

Knock at front door -

> UNCLE BOB
> Tommy can you go to your room for a
> few minutes, there's some adult
> things we need to talk about.

Staring at floor Tommy walks to his room. Silhouette of a man
wearing a hat is visible through glass in front door, Bob
reaches for the handle.

INT. KITCHEN

MAN IN SUIT looks remorseful, nervously taps his finger on hat laying on table.

Exhaling hard he slides hat to one side, cautiously pushes envelope across table toward Peggy.

>   MAN IN SUIT
>   I think it would have been for more
>   but... Jim didn't follow safety
>   protocol.

Bob intercepts, opens, shakes head looking at Peggy.

>   UNCLE BOB
>   That's b s Jim was all about
>   safety, I think there's a cover-up.

>   PEGGY
>   I told Jim that place was too
>   dangerous, it was an accident.

>   MAN IN SUIT
>   One hundred thousand goes a long
>   way, I recommend investing so your
>   son can have money for college.

>   PEGGY
>   I'll have to make it last.

>   MAN IN SUIT
>   Again, my condolences and wish
>   nothing but the best for you and
>   your son. Your husband was a valued
>   and respected employee.

>   UNCLE BOB
>   He's right about investing, there's
>   a guy back in Michigan that I
>   trust. He'll help you invest that
>   in nothing but blue chip stocks.
>   Blue chippers, that's the key...
>   blue chippers.

>   MAN IN SUIT
>   It could last you a very long time
>   if invested properly. Again. I'm
>   sorry for your loss Mrs. Martin.

Man in suit leaves, Bob sits back at table, Tommy returns to doorway staring down at floor. Peggy reaches into her purse.

                        UNCLE BOB
            Wish I could stay longer but I
            gotta' get back to the auto plant.
            Something else I can help you with
            before the drive back.

Peggy sets large Master padlock on the table.

                        PEGGY
            Put in the shop what Otto brought
            over from the plant and lock that
            work shop up tight. There's too
            many dangerous tools that Tommy can
            get injured with.

                        UNCLE BOB
            Take care Sis.

Bob gives Peggy warm hug, turns walks out back door. Tommy
follows but lags far behind.

EXT. WORKSHOP

Tommy looks down at scrape marks on the concrete as Bob
struggles to drag the 6' tall wooden Indian into the shop.

Bob shuts door, attaches padlock, Tommy gazes through window.

Bending down on his knee Bob speaks firm and direct.

                        UNCLE BOB
            Tommy, you're the man of the house
            now. You need to take care of your
            mom like Jim would have. You listen
            to her and ALWAYS be here for her.

Tommy remains motionless looking at Bob.

                        UNCLE BOB (CONT'D)
            I'm serious Tommy, you have to
            always be here for your mother, be
            HERE for her. You know ... You're
            the MAN of the house now.

                        TOMMY
            ...'Kay

Bob shakes Tommy's hand, pats him on his back.

Tommy blankly stares watching Bob walk to his car, determined
look develops on his face, he stands taller.

Bob's car drives away, Tommy gazes thru shop window, his eyes
linger on their fishing poles.

INT. BEDROOM

Curtains closed, in darkened room Tommy stares heartbroken at
ball and glove on desk, wooden carvings on shelves. He turns
toward carved wooden letters. - T O M M Y -

Calender on wall: May 1965 - The date of the 28th has
'Little League Practice begins' written next to it.

                                        DISSOLVE TO:

INT. BEDROOM - TOM'S - DAY - * 9 YEARS LATER *

Calender on wall: November 1974

Shelves are void of all wood carvings. No sign of anything
baseball related, replaced by over abundance of books.

Three 6" wooden letters remain on desk. - T O M -

Curtains are closed, a clean cut, glum looking 18 year old
Tom leans back against pillows reading a book.

Tom's ears perk hearing a noise outside, he peeks through
curtain, observes a yellow car parked at end of road.

Curious, he silently walks through house past Peggy in
kitchen, bottle of coca-cola and cigarettes on table.

EXT. YARD

Stopping at corner of house Tom covertly peers through
scraggly branches of bush at yellow 1970 Mustang parked in
circle at end of road.

Faint sound of music heard, two teenage boys smoke something.

Front door of the house opens then slams shut. Startled, Tom
looks to his right, watches Peggy turn on water hose. She
walks toward car spraying water.

                    PEGGY
          I told you boys to stop parking
          down here and making all that
          racket. You don't belong here!

RICK, long haired teenager see's Peggy. Slaps driver on arm.

                    RICK
          Charlie! Let's get outta' here.

CHARLIE, curly blond haired, stoner look wears Jimi Hendrix
shirt. Car starts, tires immediately begin spinning burning
rubber, dust and rocks kick up as car races down the road.

                    CHARLIE
          Eat my dust you crazy old coot!

Embarrassed, Tom drops his head in shame, he walks away.

INT. KITCHEN

An older, tired looking but still attractive Peggy returns to
her cigarettes, Tom stands at door.

                    TOM MARTIN
          Why do you do stuff like that?

                    PEGGY
          Making all that noise, they're up
          to no good that's all.

                    TOM
          That's why I don't have any
          friends.

Peggy drinks from coca-cola bottle.

                    PEGGY
          Don't need those kind of friends.

                    TOM
          If I had a car I'd have friends.

                    PEGGY
          We went over this. You get a job
          and earn your own, you know that.

                    TOM
          Need a car to get to work.

Puffing her cigarette.

                    PEGGY
          Don't get smart with me Tommy
          Martin, that insurance money won't
          last forever and I'm trying.

                    TOM
          It's TOM...

                    PEGGY
          Oh, honey. You'll always be my
          little Tommy, you know I love you.

                    TOM
          Sorry Mom. I love you too.

Peggy stands gives warm hug, turns to counter.

                    PEGGY
          How about some pie?

                    TOM
          Yeah, sure.

INT. KITCHEN - DAY

Looking more dressed for church Tom wears neatly pressed
white shirt, tan slacks, shiny black shoes. He rapidly walks
through room carrying school books, reaches for door handle.

                    TOM
          See ya' can't be late.

                    PEGGY
          You better eat something, it's the
          most important meal of the day. I
          went to a lot of trouble.

Tom grabs slice of toast, tops it with scrambled eggs and
bacon slices continues walking takes large bite, waves.
Peggy shakes her head as small piece of egg drops to floor.

                    TOM
               (garbled)
          Happy?

Scowl on her face, Peggy lifts broom in swatting motion.
Lowers broom, forms slight grin, sweeps floor.

EXT. WILSON ROAD - MORNING

Tom shuffles down the road staring at the ground, passes
fields and occasional tree.

Arrives at Franklin Street, exhales hard turns right.

EXT. FRANKLIN STREET

Looking forlorn, Tom slowly walks with head down to school,
cars and other teenagers pass by. Passes houses then Jewel
Food Store.

Tom slowly does a double take, notices graffiti 'Bacos' spray
painted black on white bricks at rear of store.

The word doesn't register, Tom shrugs shoulders looks a block
ahead to Benson High School, he continues on.

INT. BENSON HIGH SCHOOL - HALLWAY

Head down but always aware of his surroundings Tom's bumped
by several students. He never makes any eye contact,
continues on his way, arrives at his classroom.

INT. CLASSROOM - MR. EDWARDS CLASS

Sitting in the last row the farthest desk from the teacher,
Tom opens his notebook. MR. EDWARDS, late 20s, goatee, wears
jacket with elbow patches stands in class, points to Tom.

                    MR. EDWARDS
          Tom... how about being a part of
          the class for a change? Name the
          Commanding General of the Union
          Army in 1865 during the Civil War.

Never raising his head Tom writes answer in his notebook,
'Ulysses S. Grant' he continues looking down, doesn't answer
out loud.

                    MR. EDWARDS (CONT'D)
          Tom? Jump in anytime.

Tom, steadfastly remains looking down at his notebook.

                    MR. EDWARDS (CONT'D)
               (singing)
          GROUND CONTROL TO MAJOR TOM. CAN
          YOU HEAR ME MAJOR TOM? CAN YOU HEAR
          ME? TEN... NINE...

Several students begin giggling.

                    MR. EDWARDS (CONT'D)
          I apologize Tom, the sixties were a
          VERY good time for me.

Mr. Edwards eyes scans the room, an attractive young girl
with long beautiful auburn hair, green eyes turns around to
look back at Tom.

He points behind her to KYLE MITCHELL, disheveled, athletic
looking student longer dark hair, wears 'Doors' t-shirt.

> MR. EDWARDS (CONT'D)
> Kyle, any thoughts?

> KYLE MITCHELL
> All the time.

> MR. EDWARDS
> I'm looking for a specific General
> Kyle. Union Army... Civil war.

> KYLE MITCHELL
> General Patton?

> MR. EDWARDS
> Not even same war or the same
> century.

> KYLE MITCHELL
> He's a General. Do I get any points
> for that?

> MR. EDWARDS
> Do you know what planet you're on?

> KYLE MITCHELL
> Do I get points if I know that?

Mr. Edwards looks on in amazement.

> KYLE MITCHELL (CONT'D)
> You gotta' lighten up Mr. Edwards.
> Quit bein' so serio... so all the
> time.

Kyle raises his arms, uses his hands forms a large circle.

> KYLE MITCHELL (CONT'D)

> Earth... We all live and breathe on
> this wonderful planet called...
> Earth.

Taking a deep breath Mr. Edwards points to auburn haired
girl, wears cheerleader uniform.

                    MR. EDWARDS
          Give it a shot Lisa? The General
          part.

Distracted, Lisa turns back around.

Almost magnetically, Tom's head lifts, begins gazing at Lisa.

                    LISA EVANS
          Ulysses S. Grant?

                    MR. EDWARDS
          We have a winner, someone on this
          planet has been paying attention.

Mr. Edwards turns towards his desk, Tom flips through his
notebook a few pages, stops at an elaborate, perfectly
symmetrical drawing of a large colorful rainbow.

He adds a few touches of color.

Under the left side of the rainbow is a drawing resembling
Lisa, right side has drawing of Tom with a frowning face.

Class continues, Tom sits at desk in last row with his head
down, never utters a sound.

INT. CAFETERIA

Tom sits alone, faces the wall covered with 'Bulldog logo'.
Kyle with four teenage boys talk at table behind Tom.

                    TEENAGER # 1
          Kyle, I saw you talking to Cindy
          Stevens. She's a babe. You guys
          going out?

Lisa sits with three other cheerleaders two tables away. Tom
steals a glance at her before he lowers his head.

                    KYLE
          Kinda', I'm waitin' till I get some
          new wheels.

                    TEENAGER # 1
          You got the perfect hook-up, Krazy
          Kenny's used cars.

                    KYLE
          Yeah, my uncle Kenny's keeping a
          eye out for a sweet ride for when I
          graduate.

                    CHARLIE
          Speakin' a crazy, that old bat on
          the end of Wilson Road tried hosing
          down my Mustang again. We were just
          catchin' a bud and listen' to some
          tunes.

Tom's head lowers even further than it was.

                    KYLE
          That's unreal! What a nut job,
          nobody's gunna' touch my ride.

                    CHARLIE
          She yells about the music... like
          it's evil or something. Too
          noisy... too loud.

Tom holds breath, squeezes eyelids.

                    KYLE
          There's nothin' there but fields
          anyway but thanks for the heads up.

                    CHARLIE
          Yeah, well let me give you another
          heads up. What ever car you do get
          won't be able to take the 'stang
          down, it's all dialed in.

                    KYLE
          I bet uncle Kenny's gunna' hook me
          up real sweet, as long as I
          graduate. My pops will kick my ass
          if I don't.

                    STUDENTS AT TABLE
                 (laughing together)
          Guess you're getting your ass
          kicked.

Lisa turns, looks toward Tom, the five boys smile at her.

                    CHARLIE
          Hi, Lisa. Lookin' good.

Lisa smiles, takes last glance at Tom before turning away.
Look of heartbreak on Tom's face, he turns back toward Lisa.

EXT. WILSON ROAD - DAY

Tom walks home looks dejected staring down. Arrives at home, stands at mailbox. Gazes at neglected home.

Paint fading, peeling, several shingles missing, weeds taking over, bushes overgrown, scraggly look.

He lowers his head, continues forward, past house down uneven dirt path in field.

EXT. RIVER BY CRESCENT BRIDGE

Overcast, nearing dark Tom sits on his stump, looks at Jim's stump. Depressed, he looks around, notices graffiti spray painted under bridge. - 'Benson Bacos' -

Tom quizzically mouths the words.

                    TOM
          Bacos? What's a baco...

Tom tosses several rocks into water watching each ripple fade away. Sad and lonesome, head down, he takes long last look at stumps with 'JIM' - 'TOMMY' engraved on them, trudges home.

INT. KITCHEN - DUSK

Peggy smokes at table, has coca-cola bottle.

                    TOM
          I need a car...

                    PEGGY
          We went over this.

                    TOM
          I'll never have any friends until I
          get a car.

                    PEGGY
          You don't need those kind of
          friends. You need a job first,
          you'll make friends there.

Tom shuffles toward bedroom.

                    TOM
          Need a car for that.

                    PEGGY
          At least start looking for a job.

INT. COURTESY COUNTER - JEWEL FOODS - DAY

Large white building, bright florescent lights shine. Perry
Como music methodically plays on intercom.

Tom stands, head down at counter of near empty store. Head
down as well, WOMAN AT COUNTER, 40, long curly over permed
red hair counts change on the counter, chews gum.

                    WOMAN AT COUNTER
          Yes...

                    TOM
          Are you hiring?

                    WOMAN AT COUNTER
          Probably the first of the year
          we'll be hiring, try back then. Are
          you out of school?

                    TOM
          I'm a senior.

                    WOMAN AT COUNTER
          Have a car? It helps.

                    TOM
          Close enough that I can walk.

                    WOMAN AT COUNTER
          Try back after you graduate.

Neither one makes any attempt at eye contact, Tom walks away.

INT. CLASSROOM - MR. EDWARDS - DAY

Knock at the door -

Mr. Edward's teaches class, a hand holding a folded paper
extends through doorway.

After reading paper Mr. Edwards looks up directly at Tom. Tom
can't lower his head fast enough.

                    MR. EDWARDS
          Tom... Tom Martin.

Forced to walk to Tom's desk, Mr. Edwards taps Tom on his
shoulder.

                    MR. EDWARDS (CONT'D (CONT'D)
          You need to go to the office Tom.

                    STUDENTS
          Ooohhh...

Tom slowly lifts head, students stop, turn away.

                    MR. EDWARDS
          Right away Tom.

Tom shuffles out the door never utters a word.

INT. HALLWAY

Tom dejectedly shuffles through empty hall adorned with
homecoming decorations arriving at main office.

INT. MAIN OFFICE

Head down Tom hands paper to staff working at desk.

                    OFFICE STAFF
          No, this is for Mrs. Howell's
          office, two doors down on the right

INT. GUIDANCE COUNSELOR OFFICE

Tom stands in room looking at four empty chairs, a second
doorway adjoins to the room.

                    MRS HOWELL (O.S.)
          Next...

MRS. HOWELL, 50, heavy set stern looking woman big hair
momentarily glances at Tom sitting in chair.

                    MRS HOWELL (CONT'D)
          Well Tom, been trying to get you in
          here for awhile. So what are you
          going to do with your life, what
          are your plans?

Tom continues staring down.

                    MRS HOWELL (CONT'D)
          Tom? Are you going to further your
          education? Go to college? Your
          grades are pretty solid.

                    TOM
          I hate school.

                        MRS HOWELL
              Well, what ARE your plans?

Long pause...

                        MRS HOWELL (CONT'D)
              Join the military, or getting a job
              here locally? Join the workforce?

Tom never looks up, Mrs. Howell's irritated.

                        MRS HOWELL (CONT'D)
              Let's try this Tom, the day you get
              your diploma are you just going to
              go home and crawl under the covers.
              Is that... what are you going to do
              with your life?

Tom never looks up.

                        MRS HOWELL (CONT'D)
              Tom, it rude to not look at someone
              that's talking to you, I'm trying
              to help you, it's my job.

Tom slowly looks up.

                        TOM
              I'm going to get a job, buy a car
              and move far away from here.

                        MRS HOWELL
              Anywhere in particular?

                        TOM
              California... Northern California.

                        MRS HOWELL
              Well, at least you have a plan. If
              there's no plans for college you
              have enough credits for mid-term
              graduation.

                        TOM
              What's that mean?

                        MRS HOWELL
              December eighteenth's your last day
              if you chose mid-term graduation.

Unfamiliar surge of adrenaline pulses through Tom's body, he
sits up straight.

                    TOM
          Where do I sign?

Tom strides through waiting area with vigor, never notices
Kyle sitting in chair.

                    MRS HOWELL (O.S.)
          Next!

Kyle stands, walks into office.

                    MRS HOWELL (CONT'D)
          What are your plans Kyle? What are
          you going to do with your life?

INT. KITCHEN - MARTIN HOUSE

Standing at back door Tom stares out window toward driveway.

                    TOM
          But Mom I need a car NOW, so I can
          get a job.

                    PEGGY
          Tommy Mar.. You better watch that
          tone with you mother.

Leaves blow across yard in funnel shaped motion capturing
Tom's attention. Peggy gives him a big hug.

                    PEGGY (CONT'D)
          How about some pie? Pecan, a scoop
          of ice cream?

                    TOM
          Sure, sorry mom.

                    PEGGY
          Try Jewel Foods in a few weeks, I
          just know you'll meet friends
          there. It'll all work out, promise.

                    TOM
          You want me to be a bagger the rest
          of my life? Not the future I...

                    PEGGY
          It's a start and it's a really safe
          job and it's close. You won't need
          a car, they're dangerous.

                    TOM
          Mom! Seriously?

                    PEGGY
          Did you see the way that boy drove
          his car? Cars are dangerous, I'm
          only trying to keep you safe.
          You're all I have left.

Tom sees Peggy's refection in window, she begins to sob.

                    TOM
          Sorry, Mom. I'll go back up there
          the first week of January, promise.

INT. BEDROOM - NIGHT

Snow falls outside as Tom reads a book, Peggy sneaks a peek
into bedroom.

                    PEGGY
          No plans for New Year's tonight?

                    TOM
          You know I don't have any friends
          or a car or a job or a CAR.

                    PEGGY
          You don't believe me but you'll
          meet friends at work. You'll see.

Tom rolls his eyes goes back to reading.

INT. BASEMENT - KYLE'S HOUSE

Kyle with SEVERAL TEENAGE BOYS are enjoying a party with Lisa
and SEVERAL TEENAGE GIRLS.

                    TEENAGERS
          Five, four, three, two, one, HAPPY
          NEW'S YEAR!!

All the teenagers look happy, several share kisses.

INT. BEDROOM

Tom looks at clock, 12:01, exhales hard puts book down, shuts
off light, rolls over for sleep.

INT. KITCHEN - MORNING

Tom buttons his blue dress shirt. Anxious, Peggy proudly ties
his blue and red striped tie.

                    PEGGY
          You look those people in the eye
          and speak clearly.

                    TOM
          I want the job. Okay?

                    PEGGY
          Tommy, watch that tone.

Peggy helps Tom put on his overcoat, scarf and wool hat, all
with Tom rolling his eyes, he walks toward door.

                    TOM
          It's Tom...

EXT. FRANKLIN STREET - MORNING

Snow blows across freshly plowed road, Tom trudges along,
hears each of his footsteps on the frozen road.

"Squeak-squeak-squeak"

An older rusty, dented four door primer gray car showing
faint traces of red paint silently pulls up next to Tom.

Rear door flings open, startles Tom.

                    KYLE (O.S.)
          Get in man, we're taking a ride out
          in the taters.

Looking uncomfortable Tom squints to get a better look
inside. He recognizes Kyle, firmly holds his ground.

                    KYLE (CONT'D)
          Ain't that you under there Tom
          Martin? Yeah, that's you.

Tom remains uncomfortable, never moves.

                    KYLE (CONT'D)
          It's cool. Come on man, you done
          gradiated. Let's go celebrate.
          We're takin' a ride out in the
          taters.

Tom remains silent, motionless.

                    RICK
          GET THE FUCK IN! It's freezin' man.
          What the hell is wrong with him?

Tom flinches hearing the booming voice behind the wheel.

INT. CAR

Tom gives in, cautiously sits stiff on middle of rear seat,
he's distracted by loud humming noise behind him. He warily
turns to see two large car stereo speakers.

Turning back he notices seat is covered with strips of duct
tape attempting to patch rips in material.

An drawing in ink of a joint with a plume of smoke is on duct
tape. Above the drawing reads, - 'zig zag'.

                    KYLE
          It's party time!

Tom looks to the front of the car, sees 'Baco' firmly
scratched into the red dashboard. Dash clock - 9:21

Inhaling deeply Tom's nostrils flares, detects an unfamiliar
odor.

Charlie sits in front passenger seat, brown case of some type
on his lap, his finger slowly wanders over contents until
abruptly stopping, removes 8-track tape.

                    CHARLIE
          Bingo!

INT. CAR - MOVING

Car begins to move, Charlie, shows tape labeled 'Sabbath' to
others. Everyone but Tom nods their head in unison. He slides
tape into player, presses selector button.

"Loud click"

Blaring ear piercing music surprises Tom.

Song: -Paranoid-

"FINISHED WITH MY WOMAN CAUSE SHE COULDN'T HELP WITH MY MIND.
PEOPLE THINK I'M INSANE BECAUSE I'M FROWNING ALL THE TIME.
ALL DAY LONG I THINK OF THINGS BUT NOTHING SEEMS TO SATISFY.
CAN YOU HELP ME OCCUPY MY BRAIN?"

Tom cringes from the intense volume. Rick takes large toke
off joint, passes it over his shoulder to Tom.

Tom vigorously shakes his head, no. Kyle points relentlessly
at joint until Tom gives in, takes joint, deeply inhales.

                        TOM
              Cough! Cough! Cough!

Everyone laughs as Tom tries handing joint back to Rick.
Kyle points in a counterclockwise motion until Tom passes
joint to him.

Series of shots:

--Car driving back roads (taters) with nothing in sight but
flat vacant snow covered fields and occasional farm house.
--Tom sits rigid as statue, wears coat, scarf and hat as
everyone else head bangs rocking out to music.
--Rick changing tapes and lighting new joints.
--Dash clock - 10:42.

Tom sweats, still wears his coat, scarf and hat, music
blasts.

Song: -Rock and Roll-

"IT'S BEEN A LONG TIME SINCE I ROCK AND ROLLED. IT'S BEEN A
LONG TIME SINCE I DID THE STROLL. OOH, LET ME GET BACK, LET
ME GET BACK, LET ME GET BACK."

Music still blasts at peak volume, Charlie nudges Rick uses
his finger in circling motion.

Rick understands, begins u turn, Charlie for only the second
time uses finger to search for new tape, takes a little
longer this time seems to be looking for a specific tape.

As if he found a lost treasure, Charlie's face lights up,
holds tape up high.

Everyone except Tom nods enthusiastically with approval
before music fades, Charlie changes tape.

Placid look covers Kyle's face, he speaks the first words of
anyone in over an hour.

                        KYLE
              Saved the best for last, for the
              ride home. Oh, yeah...

As the tape plays it brings an unexpected peaceful look to
Tom. He pictures Lisa as the tape plays.

Song: -Cinnamon Girl-

"I WANT TO LIVE WITH A CINNAMON GIRL I COULD BE HAPPY THE
REST OF MY LIFE WITH A CINNAMON GIRL A DREAMER OF PICTURES I
RUN IN THE NIGHT YOU SEE US TOGETHER CHASING THE MOONLIGHT."

Tranquil look on Tom's face as song appears to end, vocals
and guitars fade. Tom leans forward quickly, rests his arms
on bench seat, unknown to Tom the tape is not finished, he
interrupts final ten second guitar solo.

                    TOM
          Who's that, who's playing? Who was
          THAT?

Final guitar riff is interrupted by Tom's voice. Other
occupants of car are livid.

Charlie furiously slams fist against dashboard, dust flies.

                    CHARLIE
          What the fuck?

                    RICK
          What a moron, you ruined the
          ending.

                    KYLE
          Dude, what's your problem?

Terrified, Tom sits back rigidly in seat.

Charlie yanks tape out, shakes's head, re-inserts into tape
player.

As same song re-plays, Tom again pictures Lisa and himself
running together in the moonlight.

Song: "A DREAMER OF PICTURES I RUN IN THE NIGHT YOU SEE US
TOGETHER CHASING THE MOONLIGHT MY CINNAMON GIRL."

Near end of song the three 'Bacos' in car turn together
holding their hands up at Tom wanting silence so song can
finish with the final 'Classic' guitar riff, uninterrupted.

                    RICK
          Yeah, that's more like it.

                    KYLE
          Sweet, the end is bad ass.

Turning around Charlie speaks in a casual manner.

                    CHARLIE
          So what were you askin' before?

Still uncomfortable, Tom remains silent.

                    CHARLIE (CONT'D)
          It's cool, what were you askin'?

                    TOM
          Nothing.

Charlie shrugs shoulder's turns forward, loud clicks are
heard. The new song starts.

Song: -Down by the River-

"BE ON MY SIDE I'LL BE ON YOUR SIDE BABY THERE'S NO REASON
FOR YOU TO HIDE IT'S SO HARD FOR ME STAYIN' HERE ALL ALONE
WHEN YOU CAN BE TAKING ME FOR A RIDE SHE COULD DRAG ME OVER
THE RAINBOW   SEND ME AWAY - DOWN BY THE RIVER."

As long song ends Tom's coat, scarf and hat are off. Tom
rests comfortably back, looks as if he's 'melted' into the
seat with the most satisfied look of his life on his face.

Tom leans forward quickly, arms rest on bench seat.

                    TOM (CONT'D)
          Who is that? Who's singing? Who is
          that? I gotta' know.

                    CHARLIE
          Neil Young man...

                    RICK
          You never heard of Neil Young?

                    TOM
          No music in my house.

                    KYLE
          No way man. You're telling me you
          never heard of NEIL YOUNG. This is
          a joke, it's gotta' be.

                    TOM
          No, not joking. My mom has
          sensitive...

Tom stares down embarrassed.

                    TOM (CONT'D)
          ...I never heard any of those songs
          before.

Rick slams steering wheel, looks ahead for a safe place to
pull the car over, parks.

Snows kicked high up, sprayed into the air as three white
tail deer sprint across the barren field.

                    RICK
          Serious? What rock you been hiding
          under? Ever hear of Buffalo
          Springfield?

                    CHARLIE
          CSNY? Crazy Horse?

Staring down Tom sheepishly shakes his head.

                    KYLE
          That's fucked up man. Neil used to
          play with Stephen Stills...

                    RICK
          ... But Neil's a rebel man, he left
          and started playing with a band
          called Crazy horse.

                    KYLE
          ...But missed Stills and hooked
          back up with him after Stills
          started playing with that hippie
          dude David Crosby...

                    CHARLIE
          ...And that British dude, Nash,
          from the Hollies. They were pretty
          good but needed somethin' extra.

                    KYLE
          They really kick ass with ol' Neil.

Rick eagerly puts in new tape.

Song: -Woodstock-

"WELL I CAME ACROSS A CHILD OF GOD HE WAS WALKIN' ALONG THE
ROAD AND I ASKED HIM WHERE HE WAS GOING THIS HE TOLD ME; BY
THE TIME WE GOT TO WOODSTOCK WE WERE HALF A MILLION STRONG."

Rick waits for response from Tom. There is none.

                    RICK
          CSNY, Woodstock? Bullshit! You
          never heard this one either.

                    TOM
          Like I said, there's no music in my
          house. My mom is a pretty good
          mother but I'm kinda' helpin' her
          out as much as I can.

Tom lowers head, softly speaks.

                         TOM (CONT'D)
                    ...Don't get out much.

                    CHARLIE
          You don't know what you're missing.
          Neil's got some GREAT stuff.

                    KYLE
          Dude, we need to hook you up. Some
          days it's a rock till you drop fry
          all your brain cells kind of day
          and then there's... well... Neil.

                    CHARLIE
          Hell, yeah. Neil Young man. There's
          days it's just TIME, for some Neil
          Young all day man.

Charlie presses select button several times.

"Click-click-click"

Song: -Helpless-

"THERE IS A TOWN IN NORTH ONTARIO WITH DREAM COMFORT MEMORY
TO SPARE-IN MY MIND I STILL NEED A PLACE TO GO; BIG BIRDS
FLYING ACROSS THE SKIES THROWING SHADOWS ON OUR EYES LEAVES
US HELPLESS HELPLESS HELPLESS."

Tears well in Tom's eyes listening to the lyrics envisioning
the day fishing with his father.

                    RICK
          You never heard of these before?

                    TOM
          I know about them now.

                    KYLE
          Stick with me Dude. I got your
          back. From now on, you're gunna'
          learn what the world has to offer.

Rick shifts car in gear continues to drive, Charlie slides in
new tape.

Song: -Old Man-

"OLD MAN TAKE A LOOK AT MY LIFE I'M A LOT LIKE YOU WERE; LOVE
LOST SUCH A COST GIVE ME THINGS THAT WON'T GET LOST; I'VE
BEEN FIRST AND LAST LOOK AT HOW THE TIME GOES PAST BUT I'M
ALL ALONE AT LAST."

Volumes lower, Rick and Charlie zone out.

                    KYLE(CONT'D)
          Where were you walking to? It's
          like an iceberg out there.

                    TOM
          My mom says I have to go get a job.

                    KYLE
          Well, you can go with me tomorrow.
          My pop's hookin' me up where he
          works. I can get you in there.

                    TOM
          Okay...

                    KYLE
          I'll pick you up in the morning.

                    TOM
          Sure, what time.

                    KYLE
          Eight thirty...

Kyle pauses tilts his head slightly.

                    KYLE(CONT'D)
          Where do you live?

INT. KITCHEN

Peggy clutches her sweater, shivers looking out the door as
Tom enters, she sees car leaving driveway.

                    PEGGY
          Brrrr... Who was that? Who were you
          with? Oh, my god I was worried, did
          they hurt you?

                    TOM
          Seriously? They gave me a ride,
          that's all.

                    PEGGY
          From Jewel? You got the job?

                    TOM
          Kyle says I can start tomorrow, his
          dad is getting us in.

                         PEGGY
             I knew you would find friends when
             you got a job. Shoulda' listened to
             me and Jewel Foods is a nice safe
             place to work.

Tom's stoned, not prepared to explain walks toward his
bedroom. Raises his hand in a dismissive manor.

                         TOM
             Whatever you say Mom, I'm tired.
             Gotta' go to work tomorrow.

Peggy smiles, removes a bottle of Coke from the fridge.

                         PEGGY
             Oh, my little Tommy is growing up
             to be a man.

                         TOM
             It's To... Oh never mind.

INT. KITCHEN - DAY

Tom finishes breakfast, head turns hearing a horn honk in the
driveway, reaches for coat.

                         PEGGY
             Oh no you don't. You're not going
             anywhere until I meet the driver, I
             need to know you're safe,

                         TOM
             Don't do this mom, that's why I
             don't have any...

Peggy opens back door, sees Kyle sitting in a older rusted
green station wagon, she motions Kyle inside.

                         KYLE
             Ready Tom, don't wanna' be late?

Kyle stomps snow off boots walking in.

                         PEGGY
             And what's your name, have you had
             breakfast son?

                         KYLE
             Name's Kyle Mrs. Martin, don't need
             none.

Tom drops his head, points to the kitchen chair.

                    TOM
          Sit down Kyle.

Peggy quickly cracks open two eggs in iron skillet.

                    PEGGY
          Need to start the day off right.
          Most important meal of the day.

INT. STATION WAGON - MOVING

                    TOM
          This your car?

                    KYLE
          Bitchin', huh? My pops old ride
          until he gets me some new wheels.

                    TOM
          Better than what I got, at least
          the heater works.

                    KYLE
          That was pretty cool of your mom.
          It was tasty.

                    TOM
          She has her moments. Wait until you
          try the pies she bakes.

                    KYLE
          Put me in coach.

Tom raises an eyebrow.

                    TOM
          You been smokin' already?

                    KYLE
          Not yet dude, but I got one twisted
          for the ride home.

                    TOM
          I don't want to get fired before I
          get my first check.

                    KYLE
          Relax, man. My pop says I'm in
          'cause he's got a lot of pull. He
          knows everyone, practically runs
          the place.

> TOM
> As long as I get a job. I want to
> get a car as soon as I can. Like
> really bad as soon as I can.

> KYLE
> My uncle Kenny's savin' me this
> really sweet SS Chevelle, it's bad-
> ass but it's so fast my pop won't
> let me pick it up until the roads
> thaw out.

> TOM
> I'll be seeing your uncle as soon
> as I save up enough for something
> dependable.

INT. PLANT EMPLOYMENT OFFICE

TWO WOMEN sit silently at desks working. Kyle walks through
door, speaks loud and direct.

> KYLE
> We're here to start workin' today.

> OFFICE WOMAN #1
> Oh you are, and you're name is?

> KYLE
> Kyle, my pop said I'm in.

Woman stares at Kyle, he stares back.

> OFFICE WOMAN #1
> And... your fathers last name is?

> KYLE
> Mitchell... just like mine.

> OFFICE WOMAN #2
> Must be Carl's son, acts like Carl.

> OFFICE WOMAN #1
> Well who's that with you, your
> brother?

Tom, eyes firmly toward floor, hesitantly speaks.

> TOM
> No, but we just graduated from the
> same school.

Playfully pushing Tom, Kyle laughs.

                        KYLE

          He's my brother from another
          mother.

Embarrassed, Tom blushes.

                    KYLE (CONT'D)
          Yeah, they let us out early, we're
          all smart and stuff.

                    OFFICE WOMAN #1
          I guess there's room for you both
          being the first of the year. We'll
          probably be hiring a few more if
          you know anyone.

                    OFFICE WOMAN #2
          Fill out the paperwork first then
          it's four hours of safety training.

Leaning over desk woman #1 angrily points at Kyle.

                    OFFICE WOMAN #1
          None of that horseplay!

                    OFFICE WOMAN #2
          We're big on safety here so pay
          attention to everything they say.

                    OFFICE WOMAN #1
          You'll start in the plant tomorrow.

INT. STATION WAGON - MOVING

Kyle passes joint, Tom hesitates, takes joint.

                        KYLE
          Guess we're in just like my pop
          said.

Uncomfortable, Tom stares down.

                        TOM
          Uh, Kyle. Any chance I could catch
          a ride for awhile, until... payday?

                        KYLE
          Hell yeah, that's what friends are
          for. Right?

Astonished, Tom looks over at Kyle.

                         TOM
          Yeah.

Montage:

--Days of the two young men working at the plant wearing
brown hard hats with white stripes sweeping and cleaning up.
--Peggy serving them both breakfast while she drinks coca-
cola's and smoking.
--Driving to work - partying and rocking out on the way home.
--Tom receiving weekly paychecks, saving each one.

INT. PLANT - LUNCHROOM

Four workers sit at lunch table talking as Kyle and Tom sit
at adjoining table.

WORKER, 50, bald head with his back to Kyle bites into apple,
turns around to face Tom, talks over Kyle's shoulder.

                    WORKER #1
          Hey Tom, what's your last name?

                    TOM
          Martin, Tom Martin.

Thoughtful look develops on worker's face.

                    WORKER # 1
          Did you have an uncle named Jim?

                    TOM
          I had a dad named Jim.

                    WORKER #1
          Sorry to hear that.

Apple juice drips off workers chin as he turns back around,
looks dumbfounded at other workers.

                    WORKER # 1
          (whispers)
          You believe that? What are the
          chances, and he's with Carl
          Mitchell's son on top of it. After
          what happened with Jim on Carl's
          old line, the whole lock fiasco.

Tom doesn't hear worker, Kyle's ears perk up but doesn't
quite understand.

INT. PLANT - LOADING AREA - CRANE

Large building adjoined to plant specifically designed for
shipping.

Carl's demoted to Loading Department, wears blue hard hat,
sits shivering 50' above the ground in a small cold cramped
overhead crane cab. Operates controls loading bundle of steel
onto flat bed of semi-truck with help of HOOKER.

                    CARL
          Dumbass, thinks I need his help, I
          can do it faster by myself.

Hooker is younger employee on the ground, wears blue hard
hat. Hooker signals to Carl above. Carl waves him off, talks
to himself.

                    CARL (CONT'D)
          Dumbass, I see him. I'm not blind.

                    HOOKER
          Dumbass, never listens to me.

Hooker strains looking up 50' to Carl's cab.

                    (to Carl)
          HEY CARL! TO THE LEFT WATCH MY
          HANDS!

          Damn Carl they teach us signals for
          a reason.

INT. STATION WAGON - MOVING

Satisfied look on his face, Tom folds new paycheck over four
paychecks he previously received.

                    TOM
          Hey Kyle, I think it's time to
          visit your uncle Kenny's car lot.

                    KYLE
          I'm down with that, you can check
          out my SS. Tomorrow's Saturday, he
          opens at noon. Pick you up then.

                    TOM
          I'll bring cash after we stop at
          the bank in the morning.

                    KYLE
          Uncle Kenny likes that... a lot.

                         TOM
          He still got some nice cars?

                         KYLE
          You can't have my 33, my pop says
          couple more weeks 'cause it's fast!
          Got a four-fifty-four and a four
          speed.

                         TOM
          I just want something dependable
          for work.

                         KYLE
          Forget that, I got him saving this
          red sixty-seven goat for you.

                         TOM
          Goat?

                         KYLE
          G T O, a Pontiac, convertible, red,
          real sweet. You'll see, the babes
          will be all over you.

                         TOM
          Goat, Buffalo Springfield, Crazy
          Horse. I guess you can't learn
          everything reading books. I never
          heard of any of those before
          meeting you.

                         KYLE
          Stick me with man, you'll learn the
          real world. You been livin' in the
          book world too long.

Tom daydreams looking out the car window.

                         TOM
          Not any more.

INT. KITCHEN - MARTIN HOUSE

Peggy serves fresh blueberry muffins straight from the oven
as the boys finish the biscuits and gravy on their plates.

                         KYLE
          You're the best Mrs, Martin. My mom
          works at a diner and the food is
          never this good.

Gravy drips from Kyle's chin, looks cautiously side to side.

                         KYLE (CONT'D)
                    Don't ever tell her that.

                         PEGGY
                    It's not so much hearing it as it
                    is seeing, I can tell you
                    appreciate my efforts.

Unable to resist Peggy bends over gives Kyle a huge hug.

                         PEGGY (CONT'D)
                    ...And I appreciate everything
                    you've done for my... Tom.

Tom holds a muffin, watches steam rise as he pulls it apart.

                         TOM
                    Yeah, Kyle. I really appreciate
                    well... pretty much everything. You
                    kind of helped me out like a
                    brother I never had.

                         KYLE
                    That's what friends are for. Hey
                    better get going, uncle Kenny's
                    waiting.

Peggy gives Kyle a slightly concerned look.

                         PEGGY
                    You've earned my trust so far but
                    anybody named krazy Kenny.

Stuffing the last of the muffin into his mouth Kyle stands,
slaps Tom on his shoulder.

                         KYLE
                    He's going to give Tom a krazy good
                    deal because he's... my brother
                    from another mother.

Standing up Tom rolls his eyes.

                         TOM
                    Don't push it Kyle. Let's go, quit
                    while you're ahead.

Tom gives Peggy a huge hug.

                         TOM (CONT'D)
                    Thanks mom, for everything.

Peggy gives Kyle a pat on his back as he puts on his coat.

                         PEGGY
              Well, I'll go along with the
              brother part. I'd trust Tom being
              with you anywhere he goes.

INT. STATION WAGON - BANK PARKING LOT

The car's left turn signal blinks steadily. Kyle waits for
traffic to clear to turn out of the bank parking lot.

All of Tom's attention is to his right, he blindly reaches to
his left, nudges Kyle.

Kyle looks over to see what Tom's eyes are glued to, nods.

                         KYLE
              Hell yeah, I can see it. I can see
              it!

                         TOM
              Got a few minutes?

                         KYLE
              Roger dodger over and out. Far out
              man, I can see it.

EXT. PARKING LOT

The two boys gingerly walk through slush from the parking lot
past the front windows then into an older brick building.

The doors close behind, sign on the building. 'Picks & Tones'

INT. STORE - PICKS & TONES

Both boys are awestruck walking through store looking at all
the musical instruments.

JOHNNIE, 20s, thin, lanky, long hair with several tattoos
approaches Kyle and Tom.

                         JOHNNIE
              What can I help you with?

No response from Tom, begins staring down at the floor.

                         JOHNNIE (CONT'D)
              Anything special?

Tom continues staring at floor in front of row of guitars.

                         KYLE
          Guitars?

                         JOHNNIE
          Electric or acoustic? Do you play?

                         TOM
          Do you have lessons or books? Books
          are good.

Targeting Tom as an amateur Johnnie seems to lose interest.

                         JOHNNIE

          Recommend acoustic for now.

                         TOM
          How much?

                         JOHNNIE
          Depends how serious you are.

Johnnie points to a beautiful deep rich reddish brown colored
guitar already having Tom's attention.

                         TOM
              That's nice.

                         JOHNNIE
          That baby there is Honduran
          Mahogany.

Johnnie picks up guitar, plays a few impressive cords,
replaces guitar carefully on shelf, with respect.

                         JOHNNIE (CONT'D)
          Sounds like that with a little...
          well a lot of practice.

                         TOM
          How much?

                         JOHNNIE
          This one's four hundred-fifty, a
          Martin D-18 if you're really
          serious but others start around
          thirty-five.

                         KYLE
              (grins)
          Martin...

Tom makes eye contact with Johnnie for the first time.

                         TOM
              I'm serious. Got any books?

                         KYLE
              He really likes Neil Young music.

                         TOM
              Feels like a tuning fork, in tune.

Renewed interest, Johnnie picks guitar back up.

                         JOHNNIE
              Tuning fork you say?

                         TOM
              Only way I know how to explain it.
              Certain music really makes me feel.
              Well... it just kind of feels
              perfectly in tune with me.

Selecting several books Johnnie turns toward the counter.

                         JOHNNIE
              You're serious. Got some books with
              Young, Dylan and James Taylor.

                         TOM
              I'll take the books and the D-18.

                         JOHNNIE
              If you want to stop by the store
              any Sundays after four, a few of
              the guys get together then.

Tom smiles, follows Johnnie to counter. Kyle trails behind,
motions in a flailing manner.

                         KYLE
              I can see it now, Tom the rock
              star. Can I be your roadie man?

                         TOM
              You got a job.

                         KYLE
              ROCK STAR!

INT. STATION WAGON - MOVING

Tom fidgets nervously holding guitar case.

> TOM
> Any chance you can give me a ride
> for a few extra weeks?

> KYLE
> As long as you still remember me
> when you're famous. A few tickets
> now and then. It's what friends
> do... ROCK STAR!

Tom's grin develops into purposeful look.

> TOM
> Got any tools at your house?

> KYLE
> My pops has a ton of tools, what do
> you need?

INT. KITCHEN - MITCHELL HOUSE

Carl's thermal underwear sags, wears winter hat with ear
flaps. He's pours coffee into a mug.

Kyle stomps snow off boots, Tom removes his boots.

> CARL
> Where you been? Kenny said you
> never showed. I thought you wanted
> to look at your SS. Who's your
> friend?

> KYLE
> Tom Martin, the new guy workin' at
> the plant with me. I told you about
> him, we were in school together.

Carl stops drinking from his mug, looks Tom up and down.

> CARL
> Martin... Did you have an uncle
> named Jim?

> TOM
> My dad. He passed a few years ago.

> KYLE
> (abruptly)
> Hey Pop, you got something to take
> off a lock?

Mug falls to floor, coffee splatters. Carl's face drains of
color and emotion.

                    CARL
          Lock! What lock?

                    TOM
          There's a lock, a big old one, I
          don't have a key, got lost
          somewhere years ago.

Carl looks relieved but still very uncomfortable.

                    CARL
          Yeah, sure. I got something. It's
          outside in the garage. Be right
          back.

Kyle playfully pushes Tom as Carl shuts the door.

                    KYLE
          It's all good dude, cheer up.

                    TOM
          Wonder why everyone thinks I have
          an uncle named Jim.

                    KYLE
          Everybody has uncles, no big deal.
          I got uncle Kenny.

Kyle anxiously drums his fingers on the table to the song
'Takin' care of business'.

                    KYLE (CONT'D)
          Let's went man. I'm going to drop
          you off and go check out at my SS.
          We can meet pop's outside.

INT. STATION WAGON - MARTIN DRIVEWAY - PARKED

                    KYLE
          Need some help?

                    TOM
          Nah, I need to do this myself.

                    KYLE
          You sure dude? I got a few minutes.

                    TOM
          Yeah, thanks anyway.

                    KYLE
          See ya' Monday then. Good luck.

EXT. WORKSHOP

Deep footprints evident as Tom trudges thru snow to workshop
door, uses bolt-cutters to remove lock.

He pauses momentarily standing outside dimly lit building, as
if in a moment of silence out of respect.

INT. WORKSHOP

Tom flips light switch, nothing. He unscrews bulb, holds bulb
up shaking it vigorously, listens to rattling noise.

Looking at wooden Indian face to face in the shadowy
darkness, Tom abruptly stops.

                    TOM
          Great... No offense Chief.

Tom walks to back of room turns on light above refrigerator,
starts sweeping snow off boots and floor.

Anxious he sits on chair, sets instruction book, sheet music
on table saw to his left. Angle is awkward, uncomfortable,
Tom attempts to play guitar with gloves on.

Tom exhales hard, breath is seen due to coldness, out of tune
guitar sounds are heard. He plays well past dusk.

INT. KITCHEN - DAY

Carrying light bulb Tom briskly walks through kitchen past
Peggy sitting at table, reaches toward door.

                    PEGGY
          What's going on out there?

                    TOM
          I'm old enough, the shop's open.

                    PEGGY
          Yes, you are a man now. I'll
          remember that.

Tom looks annoyed at first then hugs Peggy.

                    TOM
          Love you, Mom.

INT. WORKSHOP - MORNING

Tom uncomfortably rotates sore neck, enters the shop.

Several black lines are visible on wall, multiple tools are
missing. Sounds of saws, drills and sanding are heard. Tom
sits down on chair, proudly looks at perfectly crafted wooden
music stand.

Sets sheet music on stand directly in front of him and plays,
out of tune wearing gloves.

Tom stops, reaches for scissors on wall, trims off fingertips
of gloves, satisfied, he begins again... still out of tune.

Montage:

--Tom and Kyle working labor intensive jobs at plant.
--Boys driving back and forth to work.
--Tom practicing in workshop... out of tune.
--Snow melts, trees and flowers begin to bud.
--Tom's playing improves with weather.

INT. WORKSHOP - SPRING MORNING

Grass is thick, green, flowers in bloom Tom's plays, vastly
improved. He confidently plays, softly sings.

Song: -The Loner-

                    TOM
          HE'S THE PERFECT STRANGER LIKE A
          CROSS OF HIMSELF AND A FOX HE'S THE
          UNFORESEEN DANGER THE KEEPER OF THE
          KEY TO THE LOCK   KNOW WHEN YOU SEE
          HIM NOTHING CAN FREE HIM STEP ASIDE
          OPEN WIDE... HE'S THE LONER.

Loud engine revving in the driveway breaks Tom's
concentration, grin develops.

EXT. DRIVEWAY

Kyle's excitement is uncontainable sitting behind the wheel
of a shiny gloss black 1972 SS Chevelle, white hood stripes
add a nice touch.

                    KYLE
          This is the moment we've all been
          waiting for.

Tom stands smiling, happy for his friend.

>   KYLE (CONT'D)
>   Well, what the hell are you waiting
>   for? You want the FIRST ride or
>   not.

Continued revving of the engine attracts Peggy's attention,
she opens the back door.

>   PEGGY
>   Now Kyle Mitchell! If you have any
>   desire to stay on my good side
>   you'll stop that racket.

>   KYLE
>   My bad Mrs. Martin, won't let it
>   happen again.

>   TOM
>   I got this Mom it's under control.
>   I'll make him take me for a ride as
>   punishment.

Peggy rolls her eyes, cracks a trace of a smile.

>   PEGGY
>   Oh yeah, I feel a lot better now.

Waves her hands before shutting door.

INT. CHEVELLE - MOVING - FRANKLIN STREET

Kyle opens up the big block 454 engine, the Chevelle roars
down the road, backs off the gas pedal.

>   KYLE
>   Nothing on the road will touch this
>   baby.

>   TOM
>   Respect the power. Lot of torque
>   with that engine.

>   KYLE
>   I'm takin' care of this baby, I've
>   waited too long for it.

>   TOM
>   Where we headin'?

Both faces beam looking at each other.

>   TOGETHER
>   TATERS!

Kyle reaches into pocket, pulls out a joint lighting it.

> KYLE
> Got to break this baby in right.

Lifting console cover Kyle removes cassette tape, inserts.

> KYLE (CONT'D)
> Didn't I say break it in right.

Kyle turns volume to maximum setting, shifts car.

Tires squeal, dust flies behind them as music blasts.

Song: -Black Betty-

"WHOA BLACK BETTY (BAM-BA-LAM)

WHOA BLACK BETTY (BAM-BA-LAM)

BLACK BETTY HAD A CHILD (BAM-BA-LAM)

THE DAMN THING WENT WILD (BAM-BA-LAM)"

Chevelle storms down back roads at high rate of speed as song plays, after song ends Kyle slows car down to idle.

> KYLE (CONT'D)
> It's sweet all right but I'd like
> to take it for a little more of a
> road trip. Maybe up to Lake
> Michigan tomorrow?

In a light-bulb moment, Tom craftily raises an eyebrow.

> TOM
> I got an idea if you're up to it,
> somethin' I been kinda' wanting to
> do... and tomorrow... well it's.

Kyle looks on intrigued.

> KYLE
> What's goin' on in that big brain
> of yours Tom?

Tom smirks, reaches over messes Kyle's hair.

> TOM
> Yeah, I know exactly where we're
> going.

EXT. WRIGLEY FIELD - SEATS BEHIND 3RD BASE - AFTERNOON

Organ music echoes through out the ballpark filled to capacity on a gorgeous sunny day.

Tom's holds ticket stub -

Chicago Cubs vs Philadelphia Phillies May 15 1975

Beer bellied VENDOR, 50, full thick graying walrus mustache wears blue Cubs cap, blue-white striped shirt.

                    VENDOR
          HOT DOG! Get your HOT DOG HERE!

                    KYLE
          Wow, I never been to a game before.

                    TOM
          First time for everything.

                    KYLE
          I bet you been here with your pop
          plenty of times.

Tom's eyes scan up at the fans in the upper decks.

                    TOM
          We were always going to.

                    KYLE
          Serious, I thought for.

Kyle abruptly stops, noticing Tom's not really paying attention.

                    KYLE (CONT'D)
          It's cool man.

                    TOM
          Lot of things we never got to do.

Regaining his focus Tom looks at Kyle.

                    TOM (CONT'D)
          Awful lot of things we did get to
          do. Now, you keep movin' on doing
          things... with best friends.

                    KYLE
          Yeah buddy. Party on, I say.

Tom casually waves to vendor getting his attention.

                    TOM
          Over here garcon, a couple of your
          finest on the menu.

Vendor stands in the aisle 8 seats away, squints, does a
double take, tosses two foil wrapped hot dogs over his head.

They soar perfectly so Tom can easily catch them both.

                    KYLE
               (to Tom)
          Hey that last bud gave me the
          munchies.
               (to vendor)
          Hey...
               (chuckling)
          keep em' coming gas man.

Vendor reaches into metal box, 'VIENNA' boldly painted in red
across it, grabs 2 more dogs tosses them each rapid fire
behind his back. Both hit Kyle squarely in his chest.

Kyle passes money to fans that continue the money down the
row.

                    KYLE (CONT'D)
               (to vendor)
          I think they could use you on the
          field!

Vendor tips his cap takes a few steps.

                    VENDOR
          HOT DOG! GET YOUR HOT DOGS HERE!

EXT. WRIGLEY FIELD - LATER

The two relax back in their seats between innings. Kyle scans
the crowd of people.

                    KYLE
          Man, this is definitely not the
          place to pick up any babes.

Tom gives Kyle an annoying look.

                    KYLE (CONT'D)
          Now, don't get me wrong I'm having
          a great time. But... a man has
          needs.

                        TOM
        I'm not offended, I hear ya'. You
        still going to ask out that Cindy?

                        KYLE
        We talk on the phone a lot. She's
        graduating too now and I was just
        waitin' to get my new wheels. That
        scare off the babes dragon-wagon
        was cramping my style.

                        TOM
        Well, go ahead and ask her out
        already.

                        KYLE
        I'm thinking about you man. You
        stay in that shop practicing all
        the time, either there or work.

Kyle stands up spreads his arms in flapping motion, SEVERAL
FANS look on bewildered.

                        KYLE (CONT'D)
        Gotta' spread them wings man. A big
        ol' world out there. Time to get
        ya' some.

Tom's only slightly embarrassed but understands.

                        TOM
        I hear ya'.

EXT. WORKSHOP - LATE AFTERNOON

Tom enters shop, abruptly stops, walks slowly backward out of
door. Looks around takes deep breath, notices how beautiful
the trees and flowers are.

Tom re-enters shop then exits, smiling with guitar case.

EXT. RIVER BY CRESCENT BRIDGE

Sitting on his stump, guitar case rests on Jim's stump. Tom
confidently plays.

EXT. ROAD OVER CRESCENT BRIDGE

As he plays, FOUR GIRLS walk together down road across
bridge, CINDY BENNETT notices Tom.

                        CINDY
          Oh my God, is that Tom Martin?

Lisa Evans turns quickly to look.

                        LISA
          Where?

                        CINDY
          Down there near the water, and he's
          got a guitar. He's never out of his
          house.

                        LISA
          It sure is...

The girls never stop walking, Lisa continues looking back
until they're out of sight.
Tom's head is down but fully aware of the girls.

Montage: Next several days -

--Tom plays guitar, stares at river's edge, no vocals,
focused on guitar.
--Lisa casually walks down road over bridge trying not to
look interested but fails miserably, Tom grins.
--Lisa stands on bridge, kicks rocks into the water, Tom
ignores her, plays guitar, no vocals.

EXT. RIVER BY CRESCENT BRIDGE - LATE AFTERNOON

A frustrated Lisa sits on edge of bridge, feet hang over,
ardently throws rocks into water. Tom sits a hundred feet
away, fully aware, never looks up.

Tom softly sings playing his guitar.

                        TOM
          I WANNA' LIVE WITH A CINNAMON GIRL
          I COULD BE HAPPY THE REST OF MY
          LIFE WITH A CINNAMON GIRL.

Lisa jumps to her feet, runs down road toward river's edge.

Lisa sits on Tom's stump, Tom sits on Jim's, he plays very
well.

Skies darken, rain drops begin to splash on the rivers water,
small bubbles float downstream.

INT. WORKSHOP

Lisa, Kyle stand with damp hair and clothes, their attraction
is undeniable, they tenderly kiss.

                    PEGGY (O.S.)
          Dinner!

Unsure, Tom looks at Lisa. He takes her hand... she smiles.

INT. KITCHEN

Knowing her son all too well Peggy can't ignore Tom's
uncomfortable demeanor as he stands in doorway.

                    PEGGY
          Well, better spit it out now before
          I find out the hard way.

Tom's frozen in place, awkward expression.

                    PEGGY (CONT'D)
          Tommy, just don't stand there. Eat
          before it gets cold.

                    PEGGY (CONT'D)
          Tommy?

Tom moves ever so slightly, Peggy catches glimpse of Lisa.

                    PEGGY (CONT'D)
          Well Tommy Ma... I mean Tom.
          Where's your manners?

                    TOM
          This is Lisa Evans.

Peggy grabs red and white checkered towel from drawer quickly
sets another plate on table for Lisa.

                    PEGGY
          Sit down Lisa, Tom never said
          anything.

Peggy and Tom both look happy for the first time in a long
time, Lisa, looks to fit right in.

INT. KITCHEN - LATER

Finishing dinner Peggy clears dishes, serves a piece of
cherry pie ala' mode.

                    LISA
          Wow, Mrs. Martin that looks
          fantastic.

                    TOM
          It's the best in the state.

                    PEGGY
          I try but sometimes it could be
          better.

Tom shakes his head smiles at Lisa.

                    TOM
          It's always the best.

                    LISA
          Well, I should get going so my mom
          doesn't worry.

                    PEGGY
          That's right, never have your
          parents worrying but you're welcome
          to stop by anytime.

Tom blushes, stares at floor.

                    PEGGY (CONT'D)
          I mean it, anytime.

INT. STATION WAGON - MOVING

                    TOM
          We need to see uncle Kenny.

                    KYLE

          What up? Romeo.

                    TOM
          I need a car. NOW!

                    KYLE
          I heard, Cindy told me. Lisa Evans,
          she's hot.

                    TOM
          I'm not kidding, we need to see
          your uncle Kenny this weekend.

                    KYLE
          He's still got that red goat.

                    TOM
          Yeah, I want something really nice.

                    KYLE
          Oh yeah, it's nice all right.

EXT. USED CAR LOT - KRAZY KENNY'S

Multi-colored letters spell KRAZY KENNY'S on cheaply
constructed billboard behind faded beige trailer.

Several vehicles parked irregularly on gravel covered lot.

KENNY, 40, mild mannered balding man with greasy comb-over
wears matching color shirt, slacks, white belt and white
shoes, calmly greets Tom and Kyle.

                    UNCLE KENNY
                  (monotone voice)
          You a friend a Kyle's? Got a job?
          Got any money?

                    KYLE
          Lighten up Uncle Kenny. I told you
          about Tom.

                    UNCLE KENNY
          Got any money? I got cars.

Kenny follows Tom walking across parking lot, Kyle's left
behind pointing at a beautiful red convertible Pontiac G T O.

                    KYLE
          I told you, pretty sweet huh. Not
          as sweet as my Chevelle but it's...
          Tom... Hey, Tom.

Tom's fifty feet away standing in front of an emerald green
1969 Camaro Z/28 with black hood stripes. Uncle Kenny stands
quietly behind Tom.

                    TOM
          This is it. Oh, yeah.

                    KYLE (O.S.)
          The goat for sure. It's a
          convertible, the chicks will go
          crazy over this.

                    TOM
          Hey Uncle Kenny.

                        UNCLE KENNY
           I'll make you a real good deal.
           Real good... you got cash?

Tom's face glows reaching deep into his pocket.

INT. CAMARO - DRIVING - DAY

Lisa leans over rests her head on Tom's shoulder, blissful as
Tom drives through town. Joe Cocker music plays, Tom smiles.

Song: "YOU ARE SO BEAUTIFUL TO ME CAN"T YOU SEE YOU'RE
EVERYTHING I HOPED FOR YOU'RE EVERYTHING TO ME."

                        TOM
           Like the color?

                        LISA
           I like everything.

                        TOM
           Where do you want to go?

                        LISA
           Anywhere you want to take me,
           forever.

INT. PIZZA HUT - NIGHT

Many empty tables in restaurant as Kyle returns from the
men's room. Cindy slides over in booth during a double date
with Tom and Lisa.

Pizza and soda glasses fill table.

                        LISA
           I need to find a job, something for
           the summer at least, in case I do
           decide to go to college this fall.

                        CINDY
           Don't think this is the place.
           Where is everybody?

                        KYLE
           My mom can get you in at the diner
           on the Interstate, it pays cash but
           ya' gotta' work weekends. It's
           cash... cash.

Lisa looks at Tom, he shrugs shoulders, nods.

INT. I-94 DINER - DAY

Lisa beams wearing red waitress uniform serves burgers, fries and cokes to Tom, Kyle, Charlie and Rick.

Kyle loudly boasts reaching into his shirt pocket.

                    KYLE
          Score! Two weeks away on Saturday,
          check it out. Neil Young concert,
          mezzanine row six. Score!

                    TOM
          How many tickets?

                    RICK
          Four, one for each of us.

Tom panics looking at Lisa. Shakes his head.

                    TOM
          Lisa's going right?

                    LISA
          You guys go and have a good time,
          I'm working Saturday.

                    TOM
          No, way. You're going!

                    LISA
          It's fine. I have to work.

                    LOUD MALE VOICE (O.S.)
          Got no time for this CRAP!

OVERWEIGHT MAN, 50, matted beard wears trucker's hat with 'Mack Truck' logo, slams fork on table.

                    TRUCK DRIVER
          This pie tastes like cardboard,
          like this every time, gettin' old.

Lisa turns quickly heads toward table as waitress HELEN MITCHELL, 40, plump, short dark hair hurries over apologizing to the customer.

Lisa follows close behind.

                    HELEN MITCHELL
          I'm sorry, I'll take it off your
          check. I'm really sorry.

                         TRUCK DRIVER
              Everything is always good here but
              this damn stale ass pie, it ruins
              the damn meal.

                         HELEN MITCHELL
              We'll just try harder next time.

Lisa walks back to Tom's table holding the plate.

                         LISA
              Wish your mom made the pies around
              here, we'd never get complaints.

Slowly nodding his head Tom raises an eyebrow.

                         TOM
              You should ask her, give her
              something to do. Ya' never know.

INT. KITCHEN- LATE AFTERNOON

Lisa hands a handful of cash to a surprised Peggy.

                         LISA
              Like I said, as many as you feel
              like making.

Peggy smiles wide, looks around the kitchen.

                         PEGGY
              I guess four, maybe five during the
              week and make another five or so on
              the weekend if that's all right.

                         LISA
              This might get me a raise.

Peggy hugs Lisa, looks at her affectionately.

                         PEGGY
              I hope Tom feels the same way about
              you as I do.

                         LISA
              Me too.

EXT. RIVER BY CRESCENT BRIDGE - LATE AFTERNOON

Camaro parked in grass next to bridge, beautiful sunset, Tom
and Lisa sit on stumps.

Tom hands Lisa folded paper, strums guitar.

                    LISA
          What's this?

Lisa reads the lyrics written on the paper as Tom plays.

                    TOM
          ALL OVER THE WORLD ACROSS THE SKIES
          I SEE YOUR BEAUTIFUL EMERALD EYES
          QUEST SO CLEAR AS DAYS PASS BY
          SAFE RETURN CROSS VAST BLUE
          SKIES... ONLY PLACE I CALL HOME...
          BESIDE THOSE EMERALD EYES.

                    LISA
          (in tears)
          You wrote this for me? How? I had
          no idea. You did this?

Tom carefully lays down the guitar.

                    TOM
          You gotta' know how I feel. It's
          like... almost like there's a
          tuning fork inside me when it comes
          to music. It feels in tune with
          certain music, like Neil Young's.

                    LISA
          You wrote this just for me?

                    TOM
          I feel in tune with you too.

Tom stands, looks down at water then up to the sky.

                    TOM (CONT'D)
          My dad always talked about retiring
          to California somewhere. I don't
          want to wait until I'm old. I'm
          saving my vacation time and when I
          turn twenty-one go check it out.
          Maybe move there for good.

Lisa looks heartbroken.

                    LISA
          Won't you be lonely. What will you
          do for work?

Tom gently reaches for Lisa's hand, holds it.

                    TOM
          Don't want to go without you.

Lisa's face lights up, stands, hugs Tom.

                    LISA
          Don't scare me like that. I don't
          ever want to be without you.

Tom kneels down reaches into his pocket, pulls out beautiful
ring sparkling with diamond and emerald joined together.

                    TOM
          The only thing is I can't leave my
          mom here alone. She's been taking
          care of me this whole time and that
          insurance money is probably gone by
          now. I have to take care of her.

Lisa kisses Tom accepting the ring.

                    LISA
          You made me the happiest girl in
          the world.

INT. KITCHEN - MARTIN HOUSE

Peggy sits at table with coca-cola and cigarette, opens her
mail. She reads the latest value of her stock portfolio after
investing in two stocks in 1965, Coca-Cola and Philip Morris.

Current Value---- $484,173.89

"Ding" Timer sounds -

Takes a large gulp from the bottle, Peggy puffs on her
cigarette, she heads toward the oven.

INT. KITCHEN - DAY

Lisa hugs Tom, he wears Neil Young t-shirt. Peggy slides pies
into boxes.

                    LISA
          Have a great time at the concert
          tonight, tell me all about it
          tomorrow.

                    TOM
          Really wish you were going.

                    LISA
          Maybe the next time he comes into
          town.

                    LISA (CONT'D)
          Thanks for the pies Mrs. Evans.

                    PEGGY
          Still can't believe I'm in the pie
          business it actually feels good
          staying busy. Actually calms my
          nerves, thanks.

                    LISA
          The pies are one thing but if you
          need anything Mrs. Martin. You know
          you can count on me.

                    PEGGY
          You got a good one here Tom, don't
          let her get away.

                    TOM
          I'll see what I can do.

INT. I-94 DINER - DAY

Lisa sets boxes on counter, ties on her apron. Helen Mitchell
gives Lisa a thumbs up taking pies out of boxes.

Writing on her pad Lisa looks up at a large shiny blue bus
pulling into parking lot. Six men with long hair exit, walk
in, sit in her section.

Standing at the table for several moments she is a loss for
words, looks at 30 year old Neil Young.

                    LISA
          Oh, my gosh. My boyfriend is such a
          big fan, he's even going to your
          show tonight.

                    NEIL YOUNG
          That's nice... we're all pretty
          thirsty.

                    LISA
          I'm so sorry, what will you have.
          Please excuse me.

                    NEIL YOUNG
          Bring us all a glass of ice water
          first, and maybe some menu's.

Embarrassed, Lisa grabs menu's and takes their order before rushing to the kitchen.

Lisa goes to her purse, removes the paper Tom wrote his lyrics on.

Lisa stands awkwardly at the table holding the paper.

                    LISA
          I'm sure you get this all the time.

                    NEIL YOUNG
          Sure, I'll sign it.

                    LISA
          No, no, can you just read it and
          give me your opinion. My boyfriend
          Tom wrote it for me.

Neil rolls his eyes accepting the paper, shakes his head.

                    NEIL YOUNG
          Yeah, sure...

Lisa's giddy, rushes back toward the kitchen.

LATER -

Lisa serves lunch plates to everyone as Neil flips the paper to another band member, quietly sings the lyrics.

                    NEIL YOUNG (CONT'D)
          ALL OVER THE WORLD ACROSS THE SKIES
          I SEE YOUR BEAUTIFUL EMERALD EYES
          QUEST SO CLEAR AS DAYS PASS BY
          SAFE RETURN CROSS VAST BLUE
          SKIES... ONLY PLACE I CALL HOME...
          BESIDE THOSE EMERALD EYES.

                    LISA
          You memorized them already?

                    NEIL YOUNG
          They're simple enough.

                    LISA
          I'm sorry, I thought they were
          really good. You sang the skies and
          eyes part exactly like Tom.

                    NEIL YOUNG
          Yeah, Okay.

                    LISA
          No really, Tom says there's a
          tuning fork in him or something
          when he listens to your music.

All the men at the table look strangely at Lisa, followed
with long awkward pause.

                    BAND MEMBER #1
          I never knew you ever leaked that
          to the press Neil.

                    NEIL YOUNG
          I... didn't.

Lisa, now looks confused.

                    LISA
          Did I say something wrong?

                    BAND MEMBER #1
          (chuckling)
          No, it's just that ol' Neil makes
          us practice over and over and over
          and over... until he feels some
          damn tuning fork or something he
          has up is ass.

                    NEIL YOUNG
          It's not up my ass and it's worked
          pretty well for a lot of years.

Lisa stands looking at Neil, crosses her fingers.

                    NEIL YOUNG (CONT'D)
          No, no tuning fork on this one but
          it's cute and if you like it that's
          all that matters.

                    LISA
          Tom just sang it to me for the
          first time. Down by the river.

Neil's eyes open wide, takes a deep breath.

                    NEIL YOUNG
          Down by the river... and a tuning
          fork. Boy, this Tom guy sounds like
          the best friend I never met.

Lisa smiles, rushes away from the table.

88.

                    LISA
          He'll be at the show tonight, be
          right back.

Band member #1 grins as Lisa leaves.

                    BAND MEMBER #1
          That song sounds like something YOU
          wrote back in high school, trying
          to get in some cheerleaders pants.

Everyone chuckles. Neil blushes, nods his head.

INT. I-94 DINER - LATER

Preparing to leave after finishing lunch all men begin to
stand, Lisa returns, places 6 huge slices of fresh blackberry
cobbler ala' mode on the table.

                    LISA
          For taking the time. I hope you
          enjoy the cobbler, it's on the
          house.

All men form favorable expression, sit back down.

INT. I-94 DINER - LATER

Finishing the pie all the men have a great look of
satisfaction as Lisa returns.

                    NEIL YOUNG
          That is by far the best cobbler
          I've ever tasted.

All men groan and nod, they again prepare to leave. Neil
stands alone alongside of the table.

                    LISA
          Tom's mother made the cobbler.

                    NEIL YOUNG
          Pretty talented family. Hey listen,
          now don't get his hopes up or
          anything but do you think your
          boyfriend would put that little
          song down on tape?

                    LISA
          You don't know Tom, he's about the
          shyest person on the planet.
                    (MORE)

>   LISA (CONT'D)
>   He's just starting to come out of
>   his shell as it is.

Neil takes a fresh napkin writes his address on one side
flips it over draws a picture of a broken arrow on the center
of the other side, circles the arrow.

>   NEIL YOUNG
>   Listen, we're on tour until the end
>   of the year and it's a long shot it
>   would ever get to me anyway so
>   don't get any hopes up.

>   LISA
>   Are you serious?

>   NEIL YOUNG
>   Don't say anything to him but if
>   you can get that on tape I'd like
>   to hear it. I always encourage new
>   talent.

Lisa hugs Neil.

>   NEIL YOUNG (CONT'D)
>   That address is one thing but it
>   has no chance if you don't put that
>   broken arrow symbol on the back of
>   the envelope, stuff gets sent to me
>   all the time.

INT. WORKSHOP - DAY

Tom practices, Lisa rushes in flustered gives him a huge hug.

>   LISA
>   I'm on my way to work, you'll never
>   guess who I served yesterday.

>   TOM
>   I want to tell you about the
>   concert, it was fantastic!

>   LISA
>   Well, this is even better. I met
>   him at the Diner.

>   TOM
>   Who?

>   LISA
>   Neil Young!

                    TOM
          Bull-crap.

                    LISA
          I've got to get to work so I'll
          tell you at the Diner later but for
          right now I'm really excited and
          want you to do something for me.

                    TOM
          I'll call Kyle, we'll both come up.
          You really met Neil Young?

                    LISA
          The entire band sat in my section.

                    TOM
          This is a joke.

                    LISA
          I would never do that to you, I
          love you too much.

Tom freezes, huge smile spreads across face.

                    TOM
          I love you too.

They kiss, Lisa quickly steps back, excited.

                    LISA
          I want you to start singing MY song
          but I want you to keep singing it
          after I leave, all of it, to the
          very end.

Tom looks oddly at Lisa.

                    TOM
          You smokin' something?

                    LISA
          Promise me, I'm serious. First go
          in the house and get the pies your
          mom made then come back and promise
          me you'll sing my entire song as
          I'm driving to work. Just do it...
          Please?

                    TOM
          Okay, I promise.

Confused, Tom walks to house. Lisa removes a tape recorder
from her apron pocket hides it out of sight on an upper shelf
behind the wooden Indian.

Lisa rubs the Indian's head.

> LISA
> (to Indian)
> Wish me luck.

Hearing Tom return she presses the record button.

> LISA (CONT'D)
> Tom, this is going to be so great.
> Remember what you promised then
> visit me at work. I want to hear
> your song in my head as I'm
> driving. You promised.

Tom sits, plays, watches Lisa drive away.

INT. WORKSHOP - LATER

Finishing the entire song Tom stands, shuffles his feet
around the shop, stops, opens Jim's old worn tackle box.

Removes a sheet of paper, places it on the music stand.

Unknown to Tom, tape recorder is on and remains recording.
Tom plays HARD and LOUD...

> TOM MARTIN
> RIDE... RIDE ON... RIDE...
> CROSS THE JADED FIELDS HEED THE
> COLD DARK STEEL SKIES CHANGING
> LASTING LONGER GODFORSAKEN NOW I'M
> STRONGER IN THE DARKNESS THERE'S NO
> OTHER SHOWS ME HOW LIKE A BROTHER

INT. BEDROOM - LISA EVAN'S - NIGHT

Setting the recorder on her pillow Lisa presses rewind. It
clicks to a stop, she presses play.

Lisa dances happily around room as song plays then ends. She
hears shuffling of feet, presses rewind. "Click"

She removes tape places it into manila envelope addressed to
Neil Young's Broken Arrow Ranch in California. Broken arrow
symbol on back of envelope.

INT. MILLWRIGHT ROOM

Tom, Kyle wear solid brown hard hats being Millwright
apprentices, tool belts hang from their waist.

                    TOM
          Yeah Kyle, I need to figure
          something else out for a living.

                    KYLE
          Don't love the plant anymore.

                    TOM
          Never really did, only the money is
          good.

                    KYLE
          I don't see me going anywhere, be
          like my pop, sure I'll end up with
          a pension from here. Any ideas?

                    TOM
          Not sure if I got any skills like
          my dad did.

                    KYLE
          Guess it's time you find out.

A long pause... Kyle asks awkwardly.

                    KYLE (CONT'D)
          What happened with your dad?

                    TOM
          Not really sure but it was some
          kind of accident.

                    KYLE
          I heard it was here.

                    TOM
          Yeah, my mom never talks about it
          and really freaked out when she
          found out I was working here but
          the checks were too good.

                    KYLE
          So, you're thinking next year?

                    TOM
          Gotta' figure it out by then.

Holds flashlight mimicking microphone.

                    TOM (CONT'D)
          TWENTY ONE AND THEN I'M DONE GOING
          OUT WEST FOR A REAL LONG WHILE
          ALWAYS BE A PLACE FOR MY BEST
          FRIEND KYLE.

                    KYLE
          I can see it... ROCK STAR!

INT. WORKSHOP - DAY

Tom holds handful of tools, shovels, rake. He walks out of
the door heading toward the house.

Tom cleans up yard pulls weeds, rakes leaves stops, takes
long look at the neglected condition of the house.

                    TOM
          Sorry I let in get this bad.

INT. PERKINS HARDWARE STORE - DAY

Setting paint cans, brushes and shingles on counter Tom pays
for everything, looks at Mr. Perkins with a grin.

                    TOM
          Thanks, Mr. Perkins, been a while.

                    MR. PERKINS
          You been in here before?

                    TOM
          With my dad, Jim Martin.

                    MR. PERKINS
          Why sure, you're Tommy Martin. Oh,
          my gosh you're all grown up.

                    TOM
          Yeah, I remember this place though.

                    MR. PERKINS
          Looks like you're pickin' up where
          your pa left off.

                    TOM
          Don't know about that, the house is
          lookin' kinda' sad.

                    MR. PERKINS
          Well, if you're ever interested in
          volunteering your time.

Mr. Perkins eyes light up, walks into the back room.

> MR. PERKINS (O.S.) (CONT'D)
> Hang on let me show you something.

Moments later Mr. Perkins returns, carries three work shirts,
'JIM' sewn on the front.

> MR. PERKINS (CONT'D)
> Never got a chance to give then to
> him, you might as well have them.

Tom stares long and hard. Emotion causes a tear to form,
reaches out, accepts the shirts.

> TOM
> Really, really appreciate this Mr.
> Perkins. More than you think.

> MR. PERKINS
> If you're interested, I can keep
> ya' busy. There's a few folks
> elderly or just on hard times that
> need help.

Tom raises his eyebrows walking out the door.

EXT. MARTIN HOUSE - DUSK

Lightening bugs begin to flicker around fields. Peggy, Tom
stand admiring the house and yard back in perfect condition.

Peggy smiles, hands him glass of ice water. Runs her finger's
through, straighten's Tom's hair.

Tom wipes the glass across his forehead. Both turn to house.

> PEGGY
> He'd would be proud of you.

Breeze kicks up, messes Tom's hair as he gazes at house.

Montage:

--Tom, Kyle working hard at plant repairing equipment.
--Guitar practice in workshop.
--Peggy baking lots of pies.
--Payday's at plant, Tom saving every single check.
--Name tag on Jim's old shirt reads 'TOM" as he works all
around Benson helping the community.

EXT. RIVER BY CRESCENT BRIDGE - DAY

Trees are bare, Tom and Lisa are bundled up next to a small
fire. Sit on the stumps, his guitar is close by.

> LISA
> So nice of you to help all those
> people out.

> TOM
> Now I know why my dad did it. Feels
> good seeing the look on their
> faces.

Lisa, Tom quietly stare into each other's eyes, suddenly...
"Honk!... Honk!... Honk!"

> LISA
> Holy crap!

Lisa holds Tom tight, Tom begins to chuckle looking up at the
dozen Canadian geese flying south for the winter.

> TOM
> Thanks, guys.

Lisa smiles, lovingly pulls Tom closer gives him a long kiss.
They look perfectly in love.

> LISA
> I didn't need a reason, but I thank
> them too. They seem in a hurry.

> TOM
> Got a long way to go I imagine.

> LISA
> We got a long way to go to next
> summer. How far is California?

> TOM
> Let's just plan on leaving the end
> of August and not coming back. My
> mom can fly out when we get a place

> TOM (CONT'D)
> Did you tell her about it yet?

> TOM (CONT'D)
> Nah, but we should do it together.
> When the times right, I don't see
> her wanting to stay here by
> herself.
> (MORE)

                    TOM (CONT'D)
          Winter's coming and I don't think
          she's enjoying them anymore, too
          cold.

Lisa's eyes sparkle, she smiles coyly.

                    LISA
          I heard Neil Young lives out in
          California somewhere.

                    TOM
          It's a really big state, not much
          chance of running into him.

INT. STUDIO - BROKEN ARROW RANCH IN CALIFORNIA

Instruments and speakers fill the room, a small area in
corner has desk, chairs.

Band members practice for upcoming summer tour, exhausted and
irritated by Neil's quest for perfection.

                    NEIL YOUNG
          All right, let's do this one more
          time, I don't feel the tuning fork.

                    BAND MEMBER #1
          Maybe if you took it out of your
          ass.

Feedback echoes in room as Neil slaps microphone.

                    NEIL YOUNG
          Take five and get you head's
          together, you know I just want the
          best the song can give.

                    BAND MEMBER #2
          I got something right here that
          will take care of my head.

                    NEIL YOUNG
          Smoke em' if ya' got em'.

Neil, tired as well pulls a joint out of his pocket, lights
it plopping down on chair, putts his feet up on his desk.

Dozens of letters and envelopes lay on his desk.

Neil opens one after another tosses each to the side, barely
reads them, the 5th one is opened.

A cassette tape slides out along with two pieces of paper.
The first page is a recipe for Blackberry Cobbler, causes a
broad smile to appear over Neil's face

                    NEIL YOUNG (CONT'D)
          Hey boys, won't believe what I just
          got.

The second page is a note from Lisa thanking Neil for
listening to the tape of Emerald Eyes.

Looking around desk Neil spies a cassette player.

He loads and presses play, he walks back to the band.

Song:
          ALL OVER THE WORLD ACROSS THE SKIES
          I SEE YOUR BEAUTIFUL EMERALD EYES
          QUEST SO CLEAR AS DAYS PASS BY
          SAFE RETURN CROSS VAST BLUE
          SKIES... ONLY PLACE I CALL HOME...
          BESIDE THOSE EMERALD EYES.

                    NEIL YOUNG (CONT'D)
          ...'Bout what I figured, corny
          little love song to his girlfriend.

                    BAND MEMBER #1
          I bet you wrote a couple just like
          it.

                    NEIL YOUNG
          Couple dozen, imagine they're on
          some tapes around here somewhere.
          Tough to remember them all...
          some not worth rememberin'.

                    BAND MEMBER #1
          Not much hope for this one though.

                    NEIL YOUNG
          Kinda' mushy, chords need a little
          help but I admire the effort.

Song ends, band begins to start back up practicing, the
recorder continues playing, the second song begins.

Band members freeze, their jaws drop open staring at cassette
player on desk, new song plays, HARD and LOUD...

Song:

      RIDE... RIDE ON... RIDE...
      CROSS THE JADED FIELDS HEED THE
      COLD DARK STEEL SKIES CHANGING
      LASTING LONGER GODFORSAKEN NOW I'M
      STRONGER IN THE DARKNESS THERE'S NO
      OTHER SHOWS ME HOW LIKE A BROTHER

          BAND MEMBER #2
      Who the hell is that?

          BAND MEMBER #1
      That's not...

          NEIL YOUNG
      Blackberry cobbler! Blackberry
      cobbler!

Neil races for his desk, grabs phone with one hand and letter
with the other, frantically dials phone.

INT. KITCHEN- EVANS HOUSE - NIGHT

SYLVIA, 40, attractive, long auburn hair washes dishes as
phone rings.

          SYLVIA EVANS
      Hello?

          NEIL YOUNG (on phone)
      This Lisa?

          SYLVIA EVANS
      No... Who's this?

          NEIL YOUNG (on Phone)
      Need to talk to Lisa Evans right
      away it's Neil's Neil Young.

          SYLVIA EVANS
      This connection isn't very good.
      Did you say Neilsy Sun?

          NEIL YOUNG (on Phone)
      I'm calling long distance from
      California, need to talk to Lisa.

          SYLVIA EVANS
      Well, Neilsy, she's at work. Can
      you call back later, she's not
      making any calls to California,
      that would cost a fortune.

                    NEIL YOUNG (on Phone)
          It's Neil. Neilsy whatever, just
          tell her I'll call back it's neally
          important, I mean really important.

                    SYLVIA EVANS
          Okay... Neilsy.

INT. KITCHEN - EVANS HOUSE - NIGHT

Sylvia wears pink robe, patiently sits at table as Lisa walks
through back door from driveway wearing waitress apron.

                    SYLVIA
          Who in the world do you know named
          Neilsy Sun? He called four times.

                    LISA
          Neilsy? I'm too tired for games
          Mom, it's was a long day.

                    SYLVIA
          Oh, I thought it was a prank. He
          sounded like he was on drugs.

                    LISA
          Good night Mom. I gotta' get up
          early. Tom is taking me to Chicago
          for the day tomorrow.

                    SYLVIA
          Tom's a fine young man you two were
          lucky to have met each other. You
          better bundle up, they don't call
          it the windy city for nothing.

                    LISA
          I am lucky, it just took a while.

INT. KITCHEN - EVANS HOUSE - DAY

Dressed for work Lisa grabs her purse as the phone starts to
ring. She starts to leave hesitates, turns and answers.

                    LISA
          Hello?

                    NEIL YOUNG (ON PHONE)
          Is this Lisa? Please be Lisa, it's
          Neil Young, Neilsy whatever. Your
          mom is really a trip.

                    LISA
          NEIL YOUNG! That was you calling,
          she said it was some drug head...
          Did you like the song?

                    NEIL YOUNG (ON PHONE)
          Like it? Loved it, the GUYS loved
          it, the tuning fork is going crazy.
          What's the name of it.

                    LISA
          Emerald eyes! It's named after me.

                    NEIL YOUNG (ON PHONE)
          No, the other one...

                    LISA
          Emerald Eyes, I sent you Emerald
          Eyes.

                    NEIL YOUNG (ON PHONE)
          No, the OTHER ONE.

Confused, Lisa begins to sob.

                    LISA
          I'm so sorry, you must have mixed
          up my tape with another tape
          someone else sent you.

Shaking his head Neil begins to understand she is clueless to
the second song on the tape.

                    NEIL YOUNG (ON PHONE)
          Listen Lisa, I'm going to have my
          manager Elliot contact you. He's
          going to send you front row seats
          for our tour this summer.

                    LISA
          Seriously? So you did like Emerald
          Eyes.

                    NEIL YOUNG (ON PHONE)
          Listen, don't get his hopes up but
          I want to meet him when we tour so
          don't say anything about the song
          until I get there. Okay?

                    LISA
          Absolutely! This is going to be so
          great. Thank you, thank you.

EXT. RIVER BY CRESCENT BRIDGE - LATE AFTERNOON

Camaro parked in grass next to bridge, Lisa and Tom sit on
stumps on a beautiful summer day.

A squirrel in the tree above causes a small branch to fall in
the water, fish in the river darts upstream causing a ripple,
attracts Tom's attention.

                    TOM
              (toward fish)
         Don't make me come over there.

Lisa pulls Tom's arm close, around her to snuggle.

                    LISA
              (toward fish)
         Today's your lucky day, he caught
         me first.

                    TOM
         Maybe if we're lucky we'll be able
         to find a place this beautiful in
         California.

                    LISA
         Guess we're going to do this?

                    TOM
         I've been saving my money.

                    LISA
         Me too, the tips have really been
         great, seems like they doubled
         overnight once Peggy started baking
         pies for the diner. Even on a day
         I'm tired I don't mind going in
         knowing it will all be worth it
         after we move.

Lisa meekly smiles removing two Neil Young concert tickets
from her pocket.

                    LISA (CONT'D)
         I do have a little something
         special for us working so hard.

                    TOM
         Front row! These must have cost a
         bundle. These are so cool but you
         shouldn't spend.

                    LISA
          Like I said these are special and
          we're going TOGETHER this time.

                    TOM
          Kyle is my best friend and I'm sure
          he'll have tickets too but... WE'RE
          in the front row.

Tom hugs Lisa, they both race to the Camaro.

EXT. DRIVEWAY - MITCHELL HOUSE - DAY

Water drips on the driveway, Kyle stands over open hood on
his SS Chevelle.

Sun reflects off the Chevelle's gloss black paint. Sun
reflection off the shiny polished chrome rims is unbearable
to look at directly.

Kyle sees the radiator hose clamp is faulty, turns, walks
towards the garage.

Kyle yells toward open window of the house.

                    KYLE
          Hey Dad, got any extra hose clamps?

                    CARL MITCHELL (O.S.)
          Check in my tool box, the second
          drawer maybe.

INT. GARAGE

Kyle struggles to lift heavy garage door, walks to tool box,
unable to find any clamps he searches all the drawers,
reaches the large bottom drawer.

Rummaging through tools he uncovers a red padlock, picks up
the lock, reads the initials. 'J.M.'

                    KYLE
          What the fu...ck?

EXT. DRIVEWAY

Bewildered, Kyle, wanders back towards Chevelle carrying a
new hose clamp. Staring at car he never looks toward house.

                    KYLE
          Hey Pop! I FOUND IT!

                         CARL
              I told ya', hey make sure you close
              that door when you're done.

Extended long pause...

                         CARL (CONT'D)
              You hear me Kyle?

Kyle returns to Chevelle finishes repairs, slams hood on
Chevelle, wipes his hands on rag, walks back to garage.

Kyle looks bitter, hastily walks back through open garage
door. He hastily exits garage.

Chevelle's engine roars to life, music blasts, tires squeal
as smoke from tires gather around car. Chevelle tires burn
out, speeds away into the distance.

INT. GARAGE - LATER

Carl's walks across driveway toward then through open garage
door.

                         CARL
              Damn, nobody ever listens to me.
              Want something ...

Long Pause...

                         CARL (CONT'D)
              Oh, FUCK! NO... no... no...

Red Lock sits alone on top of Carl's tool box. Carl's
devastated, body buckles, holds onto drawer, looks up.

EXT. DRIVEWAY - MITCHELL HOUSE - NIGHT

Driveway's dark as well as garage. Chevelle's loud engine is
heard racing up the street. Volume increases as car nears
house. Headlights shine on driveway, Chevelle slowly idles
toward open garage door.

Headlights shine into garage, Carl sits in lawn chair,
squints from bright headlights, holds near empty bottle of
Jack Daniel's whiskey.

Chevelle's engine shuts down, headlights remain shining on
Carl. Kyle exits vehicle, stands in front of lights causing
shadow to fall on Carl.

                        CARL

            Son? Pease Son... Pease?

                    KYLE
        He's my best friend. What am I
        supposed to say to him now?

                    CARL
        It is errible accient, an
        acc...dent. You got beieve me.

                    KYLE
        You're drunk, go to bed.

Carl looks at bottle, tosses it into corner, it shatters.

                    CARL
        Sorr...y, mmm... Surry... It wasss
        acc..dent.

Carl falls out of chair, passes out on garage floor.

Kyle walks to side of Chevelle, reaches through open window
turns off headlights.

In the darkness, crickets are heard chirping as well as
Kyle's footsteps as he heads to house.

Back door of house is heard opening and closing. Crickets are
still chirping on otherwise quiet night.

INT. TOUR BUS - AFTERNOON

Smoke from joints and cigarettes fill the bus traveling down
Interstate. Band members look tired and hung over. Neil
plucks guitar strings, face is of mixed emotions.

                    NEIL YOUNG
        I got a good feeling about that new
        song, the fork is really tuned in.
        I hope this Tom kid is a big a fan
        as his girl says he is.

                    BAND MEMBER #1
        What if he's not and is pissed off
        we're practicing it.

                    BAND MEMBER #2
        What if he tells you to take a
        hike? Thinks you're stealing it.

                    NEIL YOUNG
          That's why we haven't played it at
          any shows yet, I need him on board.

                    BAND MEMBER #1
          Offer the kid a bunch of Dineros.
          Or... you can always ask the kid to
          join us on stage for both of those
          nights in Chicago.

A wry smile forms on Neil's face.

INT. PLANT FLOOR

Working together Tom helps Kyle change a belt on air
compressor. Tom sees Kyle's not helping much, he seems
distracted decides to take a break.

Tom looks at wristwatch.

                    TOM
          Gettin' close to lunchtime, lets
          just head up to the lunchroom now.

                    KYLE
          Kinda' early, we probably got time.
          Let's head over to my pop's
          department and have lunch with him.

                    TOM
          Sounds cool. Hell, let's go now
          and grab our lunch bags from the
          shack, get there early.

INT. PLANT FLOOR

Walking through the large plant Kyle remains silent.

They approach door, Printed in 12" letters with bright
yellow paint -'LOADING DOCK - CAUTION'

Tom looks at Kyle, concerned.

                    TOM
          You all right? Been awful quiet
          today. Fighting with Cindy?

                    KYLE
          Nah, nothing like that. Just
          something I been kinda' wantin' to
          straighten out.

                    TOM
          Something I can help you with.

                    KYLE
          Not sure if I should just let it go
          or not, happened a while back.

                    TOM
          Look at me man, I used to live in
          the past but it's all good now.
          The past is the past, let it go.

Kyle's entire demeanor changes reaching for the door.

                    KYLE
          You're right. Put me in coach, we
          got a sweet ass concert coming up
          in a few days.

                    TOM
          I'm in the front row...

Kyle's hand rests on the door knob, raises head.

                    KYLE
          Too bad I didn't get my tickets
          early like Lisa did. How the hell
          did she score such bad ass seats.

                    TOM
          Man I got no idea but all I know is
          I'll be able to snag a guitar pick
          if I'm lucky. Where you sittin'?

                    KYLE
          I didn't get stuck with nosebleeds
          but I'm back in the mezzanine. Hey
          man I'm not complaining but man
          you're lucky.

Kyle opens door for Tom. Tom enters, Kyle follows close
behind.

Sign above door - 'CAUTION - OVERHEAD CRANE'

                    KYLE (CONT'D)
          Lunch time.

INT. PLANT - DOCK - LOADING AREA

Concrete walls to the left are scarred with old, long scape
marks the metal hooks from bundles of steel bars made while
being loaded onto flat bed trailers parked to their right.

Carl sits in overhead crane, looks disheveled from drinking the night before. He's impatient as well as frustrated, attempts to hook bundle by himself.

> CARL
> (bloodshot eyes)
> Damn hooker of mine, he could have
> held it until lunch.
> (sips cold coffee)
> Boy, this is crap.
> (takes another sip)

Carl continues trying to 'Hook on the run' by continually swinging the hook at the cable to snag the loop on the cable wrapped around the bundle of steel he's trying to pick up.

> CARL (CONT'D)
> Damn almost! There it is, about
> damn time.

Snagging the bundle without any help, Carl, begins operating controls raising the load.

Hooking alone the bundle is not centered, it immediately begins to shift drastically, swaying hard to the left.

> CARL (CONT'D)
> Hold on there Betsy, hold on... I
> gotcha'.

Carl attempts to rapidly lift the load of steel to compensate but it only increases the speed of the shifting load, veering it toward the concrete wall.

Simultaneously, Tom and Kyle walk into loading area from doorway unaware of situation, with only a split second to react Tom sees bundle too late, begins pushing Kyle to safety putting himself at risk instead.

"CRASH!"

INT. KITCHEN - EVANS HOUSE - NIGHT

Phone rings -

Sylvia, wears dark blue dress, carries black purse and white envelope enters room while phone rings.

She dabs her eyes with handkerchief, she somberly answers the phone.

> SYLVIA
> Hello...

                    NEIL YOUNG (ON PHONE)
          Can I speak to Lisa, it's Neilsy.

                    SYLVIA
          Oh, My. I'm so sorry, Lisa's at...
          well there's been a tragic
          accident. She's at the funeral
          home.

Tears well in Neil's eyes.

                    NEIL YOUNG (ON PHONE)
          I'm so sorry to hear. My
          condolences. Is she able to take a
          call later?

                    SYLVIA
          She's pretty shook up, it was the
          boy she went to high-school with.
          The whole town is devastated. They
          were all best friends.

Neil closes his eyes, tear drips down his cheek.

                    NEIL YOUNG (ON PHONE)
          Is there anything I can do?

                    SYLVIA
          No, it's in gods hands now.

                    NEIL YOUNG (ON PHONE)
          May I ask if it's private or could
          I send flowers or something,
          anything to help.

                    SYLVIA
          The funeral is at one on Saturday.

                    NEIL YOUNG (ON PHONE)
          Let Lisa know my prayers are with
          her and the families.

                    SYLVIA
          Thank you, I'll let her know.

EXT. EVERGREEN CEMETERY - DAY

Peggy, Helen comfort each other in front of the casket being
lowered into the ground.

Carl is on his knees, head down, prays in front of the grave.

                    CARL
          This was all my fault. Oh god, why
          not just take me?

Lisa steps forward, touches Carl's shoulder. Reaches down,
assists Carl to stand up.

                    LISA
          It was an accident. God will
          provide you the strength.

Carl stands up next to Helen and Peggy, Lisa steps backward
to where she began.

Tom's sits on a chair along side of her, cast on his right
leg and right arm.

A hundred or more family and friends gather in support of
Kyle and his family.

                    CARL
          Why didn't God take me instead?
          Kyle was always a good son, he
          didn't deserve this.

                    PEGGY
          God works in mysterious ways.
          Everything happens for a reason.
          Don't blame yourself.

                    CARL
          I should have quit that place a
          long time ago after...
          This is all my fault.

                    TOM
          I wish I was quicker but Kyle was
          stronger and looked out for me
          first, he saved my life. He's
          always been my best friend.

                    CARL
          I got him a job there. Why? What
          was I thinking. He deserved better.
          My boy deserved so much better than
          this.

Flashback:

INT. PLANT - DOCK - LOADING AREA

Tom tries to push Kyle safely out of the way. Look of
desperation on Kyle's face, he grits his teeth, overpowers
Tom. Tom is forced over edge of elevated loading dock.

Kyle's fatally crushed by the full force of the swinging
bundle of steel crashing against the concrete wall.

End Flashback:

EXT. EVERGREEN CEMETERY

Shiny black limousine slowly drives in as mourners pay their
respects, car stops. Mourners turn to see Neil Young exit.

                    TOM

          That's not Neil Young is it?

                    LISA
          I forgot all about him, he wanted
          to meet you.

                    TOM
          Me? Why would he want to meet me?
          And here of all places.

                    SYLVIA
          I told him where Kyle was being
          buried, he seemed very concerned.

                    TOM
          You know him too?

                    SYLVIA
          Only on the phone.

                    LISA
          He called about my song, it was
          supposed to be a surprise. It's
          where I got the tickets.

Lisa begins crying, Neil approaches the grave-site.

                    LISA (CONT'D)
          His manager sent enough tickets for
          everyone, it was supposed to be a
          surprise for Kyle too.

Neil approaches, walks directly up to Carl.

                    NEIL YOUNG
          My condolences sir. Name's Neil, I
          heard Kyle was a fine young man. It
          would have been an honor to meet
          him.

                    CARL
          Yes, he is... was. A good of a son
          that I could ever ask for.

Tom's wobbly, slowly stands up.

                    TOM
          He was a fan of your's longer than
          I was. He introduced me to your
          music... all music. Everything,
          like he was my brother.

Neil's face begins transforming.

                    NEIL YOUNG
          Like a brother... Sounds like a
          good friend to have.

                    TOM
          He was my best friend and he saved
          my life.

Tom stands tall, speaks firm and direct.

                    TOM (CONT'D)

          It what friends do.

                    NEIL YOUNG
          You must be Tom, the mystery
          songwriter.

                    LISA
          I sent him a tape of you singing
          Emerald Eyes.

Neil looks at Lisa then to Tom.

                    NEIL YOUNG
               (to Lisa)
          There's a little more on that tape.
               (to Tom)
          Can I speak to you for a minute?

Neil helps Tom sit back down, bends to his knees, whispers into Tom's ear.

Tom's eyes begin to well with tears.

> TOM
> That would be more than... I didn't
> have a name for it yet, let's put
> that in there. Let me ask his
> dad... his Pop.

> LISA
> What's going on?

Tom reaches over to Carl, squeezes his hand.

> TOM
> Mr. Mitchell, with your permission.
> Kyle was a huge fan of Neil's and
> there's something he'd like to
> dedicate to Kyle tonight. Something
> I wrote and now, Neil has the
> perfect name for it.

> CARL
> As long as you think it's what Kyle
> would like.
> (wraps arm around, pulls
> Tom close)
> ...You knew him the best.

> TOM
> Don't know where I'd be if I never
> met Kyle.

Neil removes a cassette player from his jacket pocket, places it next to Kyle's grave, gently presses play.

Song:
> "RIDE... RIDE ON... RIDE...
> CROSS THE JADED FIELDS HEED THE
> COLD DARK STEEL SKIES CHANGING
> LASTING LONGER GODFORSAKEN NOW I'M
> STRONGER IN THE DARKNESS THERE'S NO
> OTHER SHOWS ME HOW LIKE A BROTHER."

> PEGGY
> Tom, you wrote that? That's you
> singing?

Mourners look on in support as the music feels the air.

Neil leans over, holds Carl's hand, whispers into his ear.

                         CARL
               I can see it...

INT. CONCERT VENUE - STAGE - NIGHT

Crowd cheers wildly, Neil stands in front of microphone
motioning for crowd to quiet down.

Moment of silence...

                         NEIL YOUNG
               There's a new song I'm playing
               tonight. Dedicating this to a fine
               young man... Kyle Mitchell.

Neil points to Lisa hugging Tom, points to the band.

                         NEIL YOUNG (CONT'D)
               Ride on Brother...

Guitar feedback vibrates through massive speakers echoing
through out the arena.

                         NEIL YOUNG (CONT'D)
               RIDE ON BROTHER... RIDE...
               CROSS THE JADED FIELDS HEED THE
               COLD DARK STEEL SKIES CHANGING
               LASTING LONGER GODFORSAKEN NOW I'M
               STRONGER IN THE DARKNESS THERE'S NO
               OTHER SHOWS ME HOW LIKE A BROTHER
               RIDE ON BROTHER... RIDE...

Volume's deafening, crowd goes wild with approval as Neil
rocks Tom's new song. Destined to be a classic for years to
come.

                                        DISSOLVE TO:

INT. CONCERT VENUE - STAGE - NIGHT - PRESENT DAY

Older Neil Young stands drenched in sweat in front of
microphone, thousands of fans hold up lighters demanding an
encore after a night of Neil's music. The crowd chants-

                         CROWD
               Ride on Brother! Ride!

Neil, motions to the crowd to settle down enough so he can be
heard.

Neil takes a moment of silence...

He proudly grins.

> NEIL YOUNG
> I got a new song I'd like to
> dedicate to a real hero...
> the best friend I never met.
>
> My brother from another mother...
> Kyle Mitchell.

FADE OUT:

THE END

Made in the USA
Lexington, KY
26 May 2016